IF ONLY I KNEW

Madison Torgeson

This is a work of fiction. Names, characters, places, and incidents either are the product of the author's imagination or are used ficitiously. Any resemblance to actual persons, living or dead, events, or locales is entirely coincidental.

First paperback edition: March 2019

Book design by Madison Torgeson

ISBN 978-1-7987-5982-0 (paperback)

For my mom, thank you for pushing me to put this crazy idea I had in my head onto paper and for always telling me to pursue the things I never thought possible.

CONTENTS

CHAPTER 1

Harmen

Two Years Earlier

"Dad please, just let me go," I say with a heavy sigh. "Not a chance am I letting my little girl go out with some guy I've never met." "Oh come on, it's just a date. It's not like we are going to get married or anything. We just met for goodness sake. And plus, I'm only going to be living at home for another couple of weeks until I move into the dorms so you won't get a say then."

My dad's piecing blue eyes look like they are going to burst out his head as if I just said I killed someone. "Please don't tempt me to make you live at home by saying things like that." I just release a heavy sigh at his comment.

I close my eyes and count to seven while taking deep breaths in through my nose and out through my mouth just to make sure I don't say anything to make this worse. Please don't ask me why I count to seven and not five or ten like a normal person because I won't have an answer. If you ask my best friend, Grayson Beck, he'd tell you I'm just strange like that, but don't believe him because I'm as normal as they come.

"Dad, I met Brett at the bookstore on campus this week so I know he's not some freaky serial killer or something like that. And if he is then I'm giving you his name right now so that if I do go missing or something crazy like that then you can give his name to the police and my case will be solved in no time. See I'm always looking at the bigger picture just like you taught me." I flash him my wide smile that I know he loves.

Instead of laughing like I was hoping he just presses his palm to his face with a loud grown and runs a hand through his dark hair. "You're going to be the death of me you know that don't you, Har?"

"Oh come on dad, yours and mom's life would be so much more boring without me in it and you know it, even if you only live to be 50", I say with a smile and a wink.

With a loud groan he finally gives in. "Okay fine, get out of here but make sure you are back by midnight and not a minute later. Your mom and I will be back by eleven forty-five just to make sure that you actually come home before midnight."

My mom must hear my dad groaning and decides she needs to come in and save the day like always. "Brain, leave your daughter alone and let her go out with the nice boy and have some fun. But Harmen, make sure you're home by midnight or your dad probably won't make it with all his worrying."

"LeAnn don't tell me you don't see the problem with our daughter going out on her first date with a boy we haven't met," my dad says while looking at my mom like the world revolved around her.

They continue to look at each other like they always do when they disagree on something and my mom is trying to get her way. My dad has never been able to say no to my mom and I know he never will either. They're older than most of the parents of my classmates, but I think that's why they are even more in love. Doesn't time make the heart grow fonder or something like that? I'm pretty sure that's the saying.

My mom is my best friend and my dad is my hero. Most of my friends and kids my age can't stand their parents, but it's always been the opposite for me. I spend most of my time outside of school hanging out with my parents or with my best friend, Grayson, and only friend I guess if we're getting technical here.

Gray and I have lived on the same street since we were little when my parents and I moved from Los Angeles to the small town of Mitchell in northern California. And while everyone else at school has always thought I was a freak because I liked to keep to myself and am what people consider a "tom boy" none of the girls want to hang out with me. But that's fine because since graduation a few weeks ago I have moved on with my life to bigger and better things, like my first official date with Brett Worthington to be exact.

I met Brett earlier in the week at the bookstore on campus of the small town community college Gray and I are attending in the fall. We were picking up some note books and stuff for the upcoming semester when I saw Brett walk into the store. He didn't seem to notice me right away but I definitely noticed him.

How could I not when he looked like he stepped right out of GQ magazine. His dark blonde hair was cut shorter on the sides a little bit longer on top in a way that made me just want to run my fingers through it, but don't worry I managed to hold myself back. His dark brown eyes made me never want to look away and while I'm usually not into guys dressed like they just stepped out of a fraternity with kakis and a polo, the look really worked for him.

Grayson nudged my shoulder to pull me out of my trance. When I finally pulled my eyes away from Mr. Hottie with the swimmers body to look at him, he was just shaking his head at me. We were the type of friends that always knew what the other was thinking without actually having to say anything. So I knew he was telling me to just walk away but instead I gave a him my signature smirk, okay it's not really my signature since I've never done it before but it makes me sound cooler so I don't care, and walked towards Mr. GQ himself.

He was looking at the stacks of different notebooks and folders at the table on the far side of the store. I walked up beside him and grabbed a couple notebooks while sneaking glances at him hoping he wouldn't notice, but he did. Okay so maybe I was secretly hoping he would notice, but a girl's gotta do what a girl's gotta do and I'm about as subtle as well… let's just say I'm not subtle at all.

When I was reaching for the last notebook I needed he turned his head to look at me and smiled. "Are you an early shopper like I am?" he asked in a smooth voice.

"Yeah, I thought I'd try to get here before all of the good stuff was gone."

"I guess we think alike then," he said once he fully turned to look at me and rested his hip against the shelf full of books.

I gave him a shy smile and nodded unsure of what to say. "Is this your first year?" he asked while still looking at me with an absolutely killer smile on his face.

If I stared at it too hard or for too long, I would probably go into cardiac arrest. I mean the guy seemed like a real life lady killer, well not a real killer who actually kills ladies, but one that kills them with his looks. Ugh, you know what I mean.

"Yeah it is," I answered him feeling tongue tied. I may think I'm able to talk to guys other than Gray but once they actually start talking to me I become about as awkward as a baby bird trying to fly.

"Well, this is my junior year if you were wondering," he answered with that smirk again. He could tell how flustered he made me which made me even more flustered, ugh what was wrong with me. He seemed to pick up on the fact that I wasn't saying much so he just kept talking thankfully.

"What are you majoring in?" he asked.

"Business, how about you?" I responded shyly not meeting his eye.

"Same as you, what a coincidence." I just smiled at him as he talked. That would make me seem like I was participating in the conversation, right?

"What do you say about going out to dinner with me Friday night? That way once classes start you'll have someone you can come to with all of your business questions and I can take out the prettiest girl in the freshman class." I could feel my face getting warmer by the second and I could barely bring myself to look him in the eye.

Out of the corner of my eye I could see Grayson watching us with a tight jaw. He looked mad but I wasn't sure what his problem was. I looked back at model GQ and shock my head lightly, "I don't even know your name and you don't know mine."

"Well that's an easy fix," he said as he bent down to meet my eyes with an easy smile.

"My name is Brett Worthington and I'm really hoping you'll let me take you out Friday night. Now, what's your name beautiful?"

"Harmen, Harmen Brooks," I look up at him through my lashes to see him smiling down at me.

"So what do you say Miss Harmen Brooks, would you let me take you out Friday night?"

"Okay," I looked up at him and smiled, "I'll go out with you."

I mean come on, how was a girl like me supposed to say no to a guy like him? I'd never been kissed before, let alone gone on a date. Who knew all it took was shopping for your books early to make it happen? Not me that's for sure.

He ripped a piece of paper out of one of the notebooks in my hands, turned his back to write something down, then turned around and handed me the piece of paper with a number on it. Well damn, looks like I have to buy that notebook now. "Text me your name so I have your number and I'll text you with a time for Friday this week", he said with a smile.

I took my phone out and texted the number he gave me with my name and sure enough I heard his phone vibrate with an incoming message. "I'll see you Friday beautiful", he said with a wink and then turned to leave.

I didn't notice till he started walking away that he had set the notebooks and folders he was holding down. "Hey didn't you need come in here to buy this stuff?" I called after him. He turned his head and smirked at me just as my phone vibrated in my hand with a text from him.

"I only needed to see you." I blushed as I read the

message and turned around to walk back to Grayson.

"What a tool," Gray said with disgust as soon as I approached him.

"You don't even know him so stop being such a prickly pear."

"You don't know him either Har so don't give me that. Also, what the hell is a prickly pear? You really make no sense sometimes; you know that right?" he said with a small chuckle while shaking his head at me.

Before I can respond he continues, "And I've been going here for a year and I've never seen him before. Is he new here or something?"

"Oh calm down, he asked me out on Friday so that I can know someone majoring in business when classes start. It's not like he proposed you freak so I didn't get his whole life story," I said shaking my head at him.

"You already know someone going into business, me, or did you forget that when you were talking to Mr. Men's Centerfold over there."

"Ugh whatever Gray, go get your stuff so we can leave already." He just sighed and walked away from me.

I'll never understand what that boy's problem is, he knows I've never been on a date let alone been kissed. As my best friend he should be happy for me, I mean he turned me down a few months ago saying he didn't want to ruin our friendship and I get it, but what did he think I was going to do? Join a convent? No thanks, they'd probably kick me out as soon and I reached the front door.

"Harmen are you even listening to me?" my dad's voice pulls me back to the present.

"Oh yeah sorry, what'd you say?"

"If you can't even listen to me when I'm standing in front of you why should you get to go on a date?"

"I'm sorry okay? I was thinking about something and just got distracted. What were you saying now?" I ask him with a smile hoping my mom can talk him off of the ledge he is currently inhabiting.

"You can go but there are rules just like always. Number one, hugs before drugs, obviously." I just rolls my eyes as he continues, "Always keep your phone on so your mother and I can reach you if we need to. Home by midnight. And no and I mean NO kissing. Got it? Oh and don't forget since your mother and I will be at the gala tonight to call Grayson if you need anything."

"Oh lighten up Brain," my mom says with a smile.

"Yeah dad lighten up," I tell him with a punch to the arm which just earns me a scowl in return.

"Okay, okay I got it don't worry. Only hugs and drugs, lots of kissing, and call Gray if I need him," I say while backing away towards the door with a smirk.

"Harmen!" my dad yells while looking like he's about to pass out at any second.

"I'm just kidding dad! Relax." I run back over to him and my mom and gave each of them a hug and a kiss on the cheek before I turn and walk towards the front door.

"Love you guys," I yell over my shoulder as I walk out the front door and towards my first date who is currently parked in the driveway.

I look back just in time to see my dad put his arm around my mom's waist and pull her closer to him. "Love you more," they both yell in unison as the front door closes behind me.

With a smile on my face I make my way down the sidewalk towards the drive way where Brett is waiting for me in his car. In my yellow sundress that hits just above my knees and my tan gladiator sandals I think I look more like a pretty girly than a tom boy and I'm pretty damn proud of myself. My long black hair is in curls running down my back and I even put on a small amount of makeup to pull together my whole, first date look. I made sure I sent Gray a picture just before I left to get his opinion on my whole date look and to make sure I looked okay since I didn't have any friends that were girls to help me out.

My phone vibrates just as I reach Brett's car with a text message and I pull it out to quickly read what Gray said. "*You look beautiful, just like always. But maybe you should go back and put some sweats on so you'll be comfier while you eat. And don't forget to call or text me if you need rescuing, I promise I'll come running. Love you Har.*" I can't help but roll my eyes as I read the message from Gray, I swear sometimes he's worse than my dad.

I text him back a quick "*Love you too Gray*" as I slide into Brett's car.

Not a lot of people understand mine and Grayson's relationship, but I don't care and never will. He is my best friend and always has been since we were little when I moved in next door to his family. When I was four my parents and I moved up to Mitchell in northern California from Los Angeles when my dad decided to take a step back from his real estate business.

My dad started investing in real estate right out of college which is how he met my mom. Apparently she was the realtor that listed the first property he decided to purchase and they've been together ever since. I know right, how sweet. Growing up I liked to think that I would end up in the same kind of loving relationship that they have, but here I am, about to start college and I've never even been kissed. How exciting.

I always kind of thought that Gray would be my first and last everything, but instead he apparently looks at me more like a kid sister and doesn't want to do anything that could ruin our friendship. I mean don't get me wrong that's great seeing as how I'm an only child, except I've always had a crush on him ever since we were kids. I've had to watch him go on dates with the most beautiful girls in school, win homecoming king and do all of the other stuff hot popular kids do while I just watched from the sidelines. It's not that he didn't try to include me because he did, I just never wanted to share him with anyone. I mean come on, he's my best friend. Mine. No one else's.

Yes, I know that makes me sound crazy but you have to realize that Gray has been my only friend since I was little and seeing as how I'm an only child and all, I tend to not share very well. Don't blame me, blame my parents. They easily could have had a couple more of me and forced me to learn to share, but apparently they could only handle one. So technically my inability to share is all their fault.

Anyways, Grayson is currently dating Kristin. I mean what kind of name is that? It sounds like a dull stripper name. I've always had to put up with the evil glares and snide remarks I get from his girlfriend's whenever we're together. I never let it bother me though, because none of them have lasted longer than two months. So I'm sure stripper Barbie won't be around anymore once classes roll around in a few weeks, lucky me.

So even with all the satanic girlfriends he's had over the years we've always been the type of friends that have each other's back no matter what. When he needs to vent, I listen. When he needs advice, I give it. When he needs an excuse, I'm his go to. And whenever I need anything, anything at all, Gray is always the first one to help me.

So tonight even if my date goes terribly, which I know it won't, I'm not going to go to him with my problems. I need to try put some distance between my need for him as a friend and my want for him as something more. I know he would come running to my rescue if I asked him to, but I can't keep doing that. I need to find someone of my own to learn on, someone like Brett.

Speak of the devil, as I get into the car the first thing I notice are his strikingly dark eyes that I could so easily fall into if I let myself. He's dressed in kakis and a light blue polo, similar to what I saw him wearing in the bookstore. His strong jaw is clean shaven and his hair is combed back as if he took the time to style it. I'm not the type of girl that's usually into a guy with a clean shaven face, I mean babies have clean faces not men. But I definitely think I can make an exception here especially since I'm having a hard time holding myself back from running my fingers through his hair and leaning over to lick his cheek just to see if it's as soft as it looks.

What the hell, Harmen! Get your shit together before you accost the man. This is exactly why I don't go on dates or hangout with any other guys besides Gray because this is the crap that goes through my brain. But I'll say it again, I'm completely normal.

I chance a look at him through the corner of my eye to catch him staring at me with a big smile on his face. "If I thought you were beautiful before, you're definitely stunning now," he says through his smile. I swear my heart just jumped out of my chest from his comment, but I don't see it in my lap or on the floor of the car so it must still be safe inside my chest even though I swear I could feel it jump.

"Are you ready to go beautiful?" he asks while still smiling at me, seeming to know of my inability to speak currently.

"Yes, I'm ready," I answer shyly still not able to look him in the eyes. He reaches over and tugs at my hand forcing me to turn my head to look at him. When I met his eyes I can swear I lose my breathe because he's so beautiful. Yes, men can be beautiful too. Deal with it.

I've always thought Gray was the most attractive guy I've ever laid my eyes on, but Brett is just as gorgeous but more in a preppy way where Grayson is all muscles, chiseled jaw, perfect and the most amazing green eyes I've ever seen. But enough about my best friend who thinks of me as his little sister and more about the gorgeous specimen sitting in the seat next to me and currently holding my hand.

"Where are we going?" I ask as he backs out of my driveway while still holding my hand in his.

"To my favorite restaurant a town over, I hope you like Italian."

"I love Italian!" Calm down Harmen, no need to freak out about noodles. Sometimes I swear I get too excited about the dumbest things. Even though I swear noodles are God's best gift to man.

When we arrive at the restaurant I let myself

out of his car as he comes around to grab my hand and lead me towards the front door.

"How many in your party," the hostess asks when we step up to the podium.

"Just two please," answers Brett and I'm pretty sure I can see the hostess drooling as she looks up at him.

"Sure, right this way." She turns to lead us back to a table and I swear she is swaying her hips more than humanly possible, but to my surprise Brett doesn't even seem to notice her. I'm more concerned for her safety than with her looking at my date as though he's a piece of meat. I mean if she tries to sway her hips much more she's going to dislocate one of those bad boys and that's a sight I really don't want to see.

As dinner progresses I get to know Brett and I'm actually able to talk to him without losing my mind which surprises me. The hardest part of the conversation comes when he starts talking about his parents.

"I wanted to tell you something before you hear it from other people and question why I didn't tell you myself. A little over a year ago my parents were traveling in New Zealand and were on their way home when their plane crashed. My dad was flying the plane when it went down and it was just he and my mom on the plane. They died instantly. It's not something I like to talk about a lot, but since I've been on campus a couple years there are people who know about it and I wanted to be the one to tell you."

I have to make myself count to seven and take a couple deep breaths before I can even look him in the eyes without crying.

"I am so sorry you had to go through that," I say on the verge of tears. "I honestly don't know what I would do if I lost one of my parents, let alone both of them at the same time. I know that's probably not what I'm supposed to say right now, I'm sorry," I say embarrassedly. The guy just tells me he lost his parents and I turn it around and talk about my parents who are both alive.

I reached across the table to grab both of his massive hands in my much smaller ones. "Thank you for telling me. I know it can't be easy to talk about, but I really appreciate the fact that you are so willing to be open with me and I am so beyond sorry you had to experience that." I look up from our entwined hands to see him looking at me like I'm the only one in the room. I feel my face start to heat up from the look he's giving me.

"Thank you for coming out with me tonight and giving me the chance to get to know you. And even more, thank you for letting me confide in you a piece of my past," he says with a smile. "As much as I'd like to stay here with you all night, beautiful, I think it's time I get you home so your dad doesn't kill."

"That's probably a good idea," I say and smile at him sweetly.

When we pull into my parent's driveway at

eleven thirty I find myself not wanting to get out of his car. I turn my head to look at him one last time before I get out and give him a smile. Before I can reach for the handle I feel Brett reach for my hand and tug so that I'm facing him again. I watch as he leans forward and pushes a piece of hair behind my ear and tenderly touches my cheek. It takes everything I have not to close my eyes and lean into his touch. When I look up into his eyes I see him leaning in closer. I close my eyes and feel the light brush of his lips against mine. I don't see fireworks or feel like I've been shocked, but it is the most amazing kiss I've ever had. Yes, it's also the only one I've ever had so I don't have much to compare it to, but I'm pretty sure it's perfect.

When I open my eyes I look up to find Brett looking up at me while a shy smile playing at his lips. I can't help the blush that creeps up my neck onto my cheeks, which he is still holding in his palm. I blink and sit back in my seat and his hand falls away because I'm not sure what I'm supposed to do next. He breaks the silence by touching my hand one more time and smiling at me before saying, "Thank you for coming out with me tonight, beautiful. I really hope you'll give me the chance to do it again soon."

"I'll see if I can," I say trying my best to flirt, which probably ends up making me look like I'm trying way too hard but that's because I have no idea what I'm doing.

I open the door of his black two door sports

car and step out. I lean down to look at him through the window once I've shut the door and give him a small wave. "Goodnight, Brett."

"Goodnight, beautiful."

Once inside I notice that my parents aren't home yet, which doesn't surprise me since it's only a little after eleven thirty. I decide against waiting up for them and instead leave a note on the counter telling them I'm home and upstairs sleeping. I grab a glass of water and my phone and head upstairs to my room.

Once settled in bed I grab for my phone to text Gray, "*I FINALLY GOT MY FIRST KISS! I'M NO LONGER A KISSING VIRGIN!*" I probably didn't need to send it in all caps, but I'm just too damn excited to care.

Within a couple seconds I feel my phone buzz with a text from Gray. "*Congrats Har, you played tongue war with a tool.*"

"*He is not a tool and there was no tongue either, for your information. He was a complete gentleman.*"

"*I'm calling bull, but fine whatever. I'm happy you're no longer a kissing virgin. In fact, I think I should come over and we can celebrate. What do you say?*"

I know he's teasing me, just like typical Grayson, but I can't help loving it. "*Screw off Gray. Go spend the night with your platinum stripper. I'm going to bed. I'll talk to you tomorrow.*"

"*Goodnight Har. Love you* ☺" I can't help but smile every time he tells me he loves me, even though I know it's not in the way I want.

"*Love you too, Gray.*" I set my phone down and fall asleep dreaming about my first kiss, and how I wish it was with my best friend instead.

I wake up to what sounds like a pounding downstairs. I roll over and grab my phone and see that it's just after two in the morning. I roll back over and pull my blanket above my head to drowned out the noise, but the knocking comes again and this time it's a little louder. Where are my parents, I think to myself? My dad would usually be the one to answer the door at this time of night, not me.

A couple minutes later, the knocking has turned more into a loud banging and it sounds like they've decided to incorporate the doorbell as well. I get out of bed and decide to head downstairs to the front door to see what's going on. I don't see either of my parent's coats or shoes by the front door so I figure they must have put them away in their room once they got home. I unlock the door to find two large officers behind the door. "Are you Miss Harmen Brooks?" one of the officers asks.

"Yes, that's me," I answer quietly.

Slowly the officer says something I only thought happened in movies, until now, "Miss I regret to inform you that your parents have been in an accident tonight."

It feels like my world in closing in on top of me and the only light I can see that's keeping me afloat is coming from the bright green eyes of my best friend making his way towards me. I feel myself falling in a way that makes me think it will never end, while falling into a black abyss that I'm not sure I'm ever going to be able to escape without the hands of my best friend.

CHAPTER 2

Harmen

Present

I sit up gasping for breath. "It's all just a dream, it's all just a dream" I keep murmuring to myself. Except, it's not.

My parents are dead and have been for over two years. Once I start to calm down I begin to rub my eyes while looking around trying to remember where I am. I see the stark white walls even through there's darkness still coming from behind the closed blinds. I see the modern dresser across from me up against the wall and the man lying next to me. Brett. I almost forgot I spent the night at his apartment, or should I say our apartment. He asked me to move in a little over a month ago and I've been slowly moving my things in. Much to his dismay I'm not in any rush to get everything in here and give up my apartment.

He and I have been together since our first date back before my freshman year. He really is a great guy and when I found out my parents had died he was there for me the entire time, but so was Grayson.

As much as I love my best friend he didn't understand, since his mom and dad are both still alive, what it was like to lose both of your parents, but Brett did. He knew exactly what I was going through and we sort of became each other's person to lean on since neither of us had anyone else. Both of my parents were only children and my grandparents on both sides passed away while I was still in high school. Which left me with no one other than my best friend and boyfriend.

After my parents' deaths I learned that apparently Brett's parents were both estranged from their families so he'd never met any of them. Because of that we are more alike than I even thought we would be, he knew what I was going through better than anyone else I could talk to. It gave me a sense of comfort from the very beginning to know that even though my parents were gone and it was a tragic accident, I wasn't the only one who has had to deal with that kind of situation. It helped me take a step back and realize I'm not alone.

Even if we are perfect for each other in that aspect, sometimes it seems like that is the only reason we are still together. I mean don't get me wrong Brett's a great guy. Tall, muscular, smart and generously handsome. I know I only listed things on the outside but on the inside he really is a great guy. Sometimes he seems to have a short fuse with me, which is strange because he's never like that with anyone else.

I always try not to worry about it though because I don't mind. I mean, I probably should since we've been together for over two years, but I don't. I almost like it when he gets mad at me because I think maybe this time we will breakup. The relief I feel just thinking about him breaking up with me should probably be a big red flag on my part, but since the beginning I've been too afraid to ever do it myself.

It's not that I'm afraid of him or really even afraid of losing him, it's more the idea of him I don't want to lose. If he leaves me then I truly have no one who understands what I went through with my parents and am still going through a couple years later. Gray is my best friend and always will be, but he doesn't understand me like Brett does and I'm just scared if I lose him I may never find someone who does again.

Over the years we've exchanged "I love yous", but if I'm being honest with myself I don't think I've ever meant it. I meant it when I used to say it in my head to Gray all the time, but he's my best friend so nothing can ever change. He's always with different girls, just like in high school so I've decided my best bet is to stay with Brett until he doesn't want me anymore. I know that probably sounds like I'm selling myself short, but the truth is after my parents died I've had no real desire to get close to anyone in that sense anymore.

Speaking of that someone I shared a bed with last night, my thoughts are cut short by movement to my left. Brett rolls over to face me and gives me a small smile. "Good morning, beautiful."

"Good morning, did I wake you?"

"No not at all, I need to get up and head into work anyways."

After getting his Masters Degree last year, Brett got a job at a law office in town learning under one of their top lawyers. He decided last year that he wanted to pursue a career in law, so as of late he has been applying for different law schools in the area. He doesn't know if he'll get into one based on his grades alone but he hopes that with a recommendation one of the lawyers from the firm he's working for, they will give him a chance.

I'm in my senior year right now and I still don't really know what I want to do once I graduate. After my parents died I was told multiple times that people usually deal with grief in one of two ways. One, the person finds themselves falling behind in most aspects of their lives. Or two, they try to push away the pain they're feeling by putting all of their focus on one thing. I guess you could say I dealt with my grief the second of the two ways. When I started my freshman year I didn't think I'd be able to handle it so soon after their passing, but instead I found myself working harder than I ever had before. I took as many credits as I possibly could each semester since then and because of that I will be graduating a year early with Gray, and get my business degree.

My first class starts at eight, but per tradition and routine, Gray and I get breakfast together almost every morning. It's something we've done since freshman year and something we plan to continue until we graduate in the spring. We will both be graduating with our business degree even though Gray is a year older than me at twenty-two. You'd think that based on how he likes to talk about how he is so much more mature than me that he'd be at least two or three years older than me, but nope. He's a measly year older and he will never let me forget it.

So every time we go out and get breakfast together since he is so much older than me it's my rule that he always pays for our food. And let's be real, if we ever go out for lunch or dinner I make him pay for that too. I mean come on, I'm a poor twenty-one-year-old and he's a much older twenty-two-year old so obviously he has the funds to support us both, food wise at least.

Fine, so yes I have money, a lot of money to be exact. After my parents died I learned that my dad was a lot bigger in the real estate game than I ever knew. My parents never talked about work at night when we were all together. My mom always liked for us to focus on each other when we were together rather than complaining about our days.

Don't get me wrong, we all complained at some point or another, but for the most part we were a pretty positive and loving family. She always said to leave your problems at the front door, along with work, so that's what they did. Neither of them discussed their jobs at home much unless I was out of the room and happened to eavesdrop on them. They always said they never wanted me to worry, they wanted me to live a carefree childhood because that's what I deserved.

Smiling to myself at the memory, I looked up when I heard Brett come out of the bathroom. "What are you smiling about?" he asks with a hit of annoyance.

"My parents," I answer simply. In the past two years I had found myself smiling a lot more rather than crying whenever I thought about them.

"Okay and why were you smiling? Aren't you supposed to be crying still when you think about them?" He always made me feel so guilty for how I grieved my parents. I know most people probably wouldn't put up with it, but they just don't understand what it's like to suddenly lose both of your parents on the same day you go on your first date with someone who also lost both their parents suddenly.

I typically don't believe in all that fate bullshit, but when it comes to Brett I really don't think there's any other explanation. We may not be perfect together and fight a lot, but at the end of the day our similar pasts and experiences make us perfect for each other in my eyes.

I used to think that I would end up with Gray one day, besides the fact that he is blatantly attractive with his full head of dark brown hair, green eyes, chiseled jaw and a body made for sin – if you were into that kind of thing – he's sweet and kind and above all he's my best friend. I may still have a couple hidden feelings buried deep down, but no one needs to know that besides me, myself and I of course.

It would never work anyways, at least that's what Brett tells me every time we get in a fight. "No one will ever understand you like I do, beautiful. You and I are meant to be together forever. How else can you explain us finding each other and our shared experiences?"

He's always so believable and sweet when he wants to be but then there are times when I'm not too sure why I stay. But all it takes is me thinking back to that summer night over two years ago to remember why we are still together. He comforted me and in a way that no one else could and I will always be grateful to him for that.

"Focus Harmen," I say to myself while silently shaking my head. Ugh, I always get lost in thought while I'm talking to Brett.

"Are you even listening to me?" he asks with a huff.

"Yeah, I'm sorry I was just thinking about something."

"You're always thinking about something

else while I'm talking to you and it pisses me off."

"Look I'm sorry okay? I really am," I try to give him my form of puppy dog eyes. Lip out. Chin down. And then I look up at him through my long black lashes. I think it's a pretty good face and I'm almost positive it makes me look like an absolute angel, even though it never does me any good. I still try cause why the hell not.

"Don't make that face, you know it doesn't suit you." See I told you it never works.

"I really am sorry Brett. Just tell me what you were saying so you're not late for work," I say with a cautious smile.

"Never mind. It doesn't matter. I'll see you later tonight. You're coming over again right and bringing more of your stuff?"

"Actually I have plans to go out to eat with Grayson tonight. So I might not be able to grab more things, but I will stay here."

"What?" he asks with a pause.

"Why is it okay for you to go out on dates with him but I can't with other girls?"

I'm pretty sure my mouth is laying on the ground by my feet as I stare at him with wide eyes. "I know you aren't the biggest fan of Gray, but he's my best friend so I'm going to go have dinner with him. But let me be clear. It's not a date. It's dinner. With a friend. That's it."

"Yeah a friend who wants what's mine," he says with a growl.

Usually I would find his possessive tone attractive, but not when it comes to Grayson. No one will ever tell me what I'm allowed to do when it comes to him. "If it's that big of a deal then go out with a girl that's just a friend. I don't care." I honestly didn't care, that was the sad part.

"I don't want to go out with other girls, but I will if you keep going out with Grayson. How do you think it looks when my friends see you out having "dinner" with him?" He seriously just used air quotes. How old is he, four? Dinner is dinner. No air quotes are needed.

"I'm sorry okay, but I'm not going to cut Gray out of my life. I know that makes you upset, but I just won't do it." I knew I would have to compromise somehow in order to get him to calm down. So with a sigh I said," But I won't hangout with him as much anymore if it really upsets you okay?" I looked up to see him smiling at me.

"That's all I ask. Thank you, Beautiful," he says as he leans down to kiss my cheek.

"I have to go, but I'll see you again tonight. Love you," he says over his shoulder as he makes his way to the door.

"Love you too," I answer even though I'm not sure I really mean it.

CHAPTER 3

Grayson

"Finally. What took you so long," I said to Harmen as she walked into the small corner dinner we eat breakfast at most mornings.

"I stayed at Brett's last night, like normal, but it got a little heated this morning before he left." I could immediately feel my jaw clench almost involuntarily. I obviously clenched it a little bit myself, but it did it mostly on its own. Freaky, I know.

It's like I can't control how my body reacts to her. I used to be able to control it when we were younger, mainly because I didn't know I was in love with her back then. I know I can't say anything to her about it because she obviously doesn't feel the same way anymore, which is why she's with that tool shop.

If anyone knew Harmen the way, I do they would have a hard time not falling in love with her too. I can honestly say I've never met or seen anyone as beautiful as my best friend. She has a pair of crystal blue doe eyes that steal me breathe away every time I look into them. Paired with her lean body, porcelain skin, straight nose and long black hair she stops traffic every time she crosses the street and the best part is that she doesn't even know it.

I've felt the same way about her ever since we were kids, I just didn't understand the depth of my feelings until she started dated Brett. In high school I knew I liked her as more than just my best friend and if I'm being completely honest, I probably loved her then too. But in the face of our friendship I dated pretty much anything that moved just to try distract me at least a little from my best friend.

Ever since she got with Brett right before her parent's deaths I've had a hard time keeping my feelings in check around her. All I want to do is tell her to leave that loser and pick me because I've finally pulled my head out of my ass, but I know that won't happen, at least not with Brett still around and maybe not ever.

I've never liked the guy, but for some unforeseen reason Harmen does. Ever since we first saw him in the bookstore a couple years ago I've had a weird feeling about him. I've never been able to put my finger on it but there's just something about him that makes me question everything he says and does. And no it's not the fact that he's with the girl I love either, okay fine maybe that has a little something to do with it.

"Good lord Harmen LeAnn, I do not want to lose my breakfast from hearing about it getting heated with him. Ugh, I'm going to need some peroxide to clean out my ears after hearing that," I groaned dramatically.

"Oh shut the hell up, it wasn't that kind of heated. Get your head out of the gutter for two minutes if you can manage it." I only used her full and middle name to piss her off because I know she hates it, which makes it that much more enjoyable for me.

"Fine, I pulled it out. I'm listening, what got heated?"

"I told Brett about our dinner tonight and he didn't take it very well," she nervously chews on her lip after she speaks. That's her tell, whenever she gets nervous or is feeling guilty about something she will chew on her bottom lip like it was a piece of licorice. She tends to do it a lot when she talks about what's his nuts. I'm not sure what puts her so on edge everything we talk about him, but I don't like it.

"What do you mean he didn't take it very well? We always go to dinner. Just like we always have breakfast. It's our thing."

"I know that's what I told him, but he just got upset and said that people probably think you and I are the ones in a relationship since we go on so many dates."

Now there's a marvelous idea, Harmen and I dating. I wonder what she would think of that idea. "I told him they're not dates," she says with a laugh. "I mean come on you and I dating, where does he get these ideas."

Okay well I guess that answers my question. Apparently the idea of us dating is laughable to her. And this is exactly why I've kept my feelings to myself after the stunt she pulled senior year, at least the best I can.

If I'm not able to have Harmen as a girlfriend of sorts, then I will settle for just having her as a friend because I don't ever want to go a day without having her in my life in some type of capacity. But I also don't like the idea of giving up time with her just to appease Malibu Ken doll.

"So what, we don't get to hangout anymore?" I ask with a little bit of hesitation.

"What? No! I told him that he can't stop me from seeing you, I mean come on we're best friends. We just have to rein in our dinners and maybe not have breakfast quite so often", she answers looking like it was hard for her to say.

"Why? We've been doing breakfast almost every morning since we were little. We've only missed a day if we were sick and even then we tried not to miss. Why are you willing to change that for him, Har?"

I can't believe my best friend is willing to change our traditions like they never existed for some guy. I can tell she's getting upset with my constant question, but I mean seriously come on. I'm not going to let that scum bucket take my best friend away from me. He already has her heart; he's not getting all of her time too. Not going to happen.

"I'm compromising with my boyfriend. That's all I'm doing and I really hoped my best friend would understand that." She is trying so hard to hide how upset she is, but she can't hide anything from me. She bounces her right leg every time she gets upset. I honestly don't think she knows she does it, but I can tell that right now her leg in bouncing under the table because her upper body is also bouncing along with it and it wasn't doing that before we started this conversation.

It's not that I'm trying to upset her, I would never intentionally want to hurt her but she needs to see how ludicrous this is. I don't care how long they've been together; we've been together longer. Obviously just as friends, but still.

"I do understand that Har. You know all I want is for you to be happy, but I don't think giving up on our friendship will make you happy. Am I wrong?" I look at her as she rolls those gorgeous eyes just to show me how annoyed of my questions she is.

"No you're not wrong. That's why I said we just can't have dinner and breakfast every day. I never said we still can't hang out and get breakfast every couple days or something. I don't get why you're getting so upset about this," she asks with a furrowed brow.

"Seriously? You don't understand why I'm

getting upset over this? Are you really that dense sometimes?" Shit I didn't mean to say that out loud, now she's going to give it to me good.

"What the hell Grayson! I'm not dense and you know that so don't be an asshole because the world doesn't always revolve around you," she says with fire in her eyes followed up by dramatically crossing her arms over her chest.

I put my hands up in defense to try ward off the fire breathing dragon that is going to take over my best friend if she gets more upset. "Okay, okay I'm sorry alright? I just don't like the idea of anybody taking my best friend away from me, especially not him."

"He has a name Gray, so use it."

I let out a heavy sigh before replying, "Ugh fine. I don't want to lose my best friend to Brett. There ya happy now? I said his name."

"Much better, thank you," she answers with a smug smile and only a minimal amount of smoke coming out of her ears. Apparently the dragon has been contained, at least for now.

I really can't say no to her. I swear it's impossible. No matter how hard I try she looks at me with those big doe eyes and I practically fall at her feet willing to give her anything she wants. I really need to work on that.

As I look at her sitting across from me I realize just how truly afraid I am of him taking over all of her time. I know the guy doesn't like me, he's never been secretive about that fact and I've replicated his feelings from day one so it's no big deal. But why is he all of a sudden trying to convince her that we need to see each other less?

I don't get what's changed. I doubt she knows either, but I might as well ask her. What's the worst that could happen? She gets mad at me? Eh, I'm not too worried she's never been able to be upset with me for very long anyways.

"I just have to asked Har, what's changed? A couple months ago he didn't give a rat's ass that you and I were getting breakfast all the time or going out to dinner every once in a while. So what gives, why now?"

"I don't know Gray, but I agree with what he was saying this morning. He thinks it looks bad when people see you and I out together all the time, it looks bad for him and I don't want to do that to him. I know he wouldn't do anything to intentionally make me look bad so I don't want to do the same thing to him." Oh you've got to be shitting me. She's going along with this nonsense because she doesn't want him to look bad? Come on.

"He doesn't make you look bad, really Harmen? How about all of the times he makes you feel like crap about being upset because you lost your parents? Or how about all of the times he freaks out about the smallest things, like you leaving garbage in his car? I mean come on, the dude acts more like a chick than you do with the stuff he gets upset about." I take a deep breath after my monologue and hope I don't come face to face with the dragon. The on lookers at the café will have to whip out some swords and run for cover if she emerges.

Oh lord almighty is that smoke coming out of her ears? That's not a good sign. I thought I got rid of that earlier. "Knock it off Gray. I'm sick of you talking about our relationship like he walks all over me. He doesn't. I don't know what it is you hate about Brett and my relationship so much, but you really need to get over it before we will be missing more than just a couple meals. I'm serious Grayson. Get over it or I'm out of here." She was a full fledge dragon now and I can feel myself about to begin breathing fire right back.

"Get over it seriously? Fine I'm over it. Excuse me for wanting what's best for my friend, especially when I know it's not him, and for not wanting to give up our time together. Didn't know it was a crime to care about you Har." Now I'm fuming. I mean seriously, the guy is a snake and yet she doesn't see it.

I honestly feel like I'm going to lose my best friend to someone I know isn't right for her. I don't know what else I can say or do to get her to see what I see. To see him how I do. It's not even that I want her for myself, don't get me wrong I absolutely do, but I also want what's best for her and I know that low life isn't it. He might look great on the outside, but on the inside he's more vile than anyone I've ever met.

The screech of a chair pulls me out of my internal monologue. I look up to see my dragon queen stand up and look at me with an amount fire in her eyes I haven't seen there before. "I know you care about me Gray, but you aren't my dad or my brother for that matter so I don't want to hear it. You don't know what's best for me, I know you think you do but you aren't my keeper, you're supposed to be my best friend so until you start acting like it don't talk to me. Let me know when you're ready to support me and maybe I won't be so unbelievably pissed at you by then."

With that she forcefully pushes her chair back in, hastily turns on her heels and exits the café. She has always been a bit over dramatic if you ask me. I decide I'll give her a couple hours to cool off, by then she'll be back to her human form.

I grab our ticket the waitress left and head to the front to pay for our breakfast and see that we had apparently gathered an audience with our medieval show down.

After paying for our food and making my way out of the café and onto the sidewalk out front I almost expect to see Harmen standing outside waiting for me like she usually is after we fight, but instead I'm met with a cool breeze and no sight of my best friend. Like I said before, I'll give her a couple hours to cool down and then everything will be as good as new, just like it always is.

CHAPTER 4

Harmen

Ugh what an asshole! I can't believe the balls that man has. What gives him the right to talk about my relationship like it's a sham, like Brett is walking all over me. He's the sham. He has no idea what he's talking about. Yes, Brett and I may not have the perfect relationship but it's built on honestly and trust and there's nothing more important than that in a relationship.

Brett and I started our relationship on the worst day of my life and he's been there for me every day since then. Obviously we've had a couple hiccups, hit a few bumps along the way, but we are just as strong as ever. I may not know if I'm completely in love with him like he says he is with me, but I'm starting to think that Gray isn't the one for me like I have always thought he was.

After all my classes are done I make my way home to get ready to spend the night with Brett again. I pull out my phone and see that I have four missed calls and three text messages from Gray.

Each one varying from him saying he's sorry that he upset me but that he was just trying to look out for me, to how he knows Brett isn't the guy for me. Blah Blah Blah. I don't care what he says, I'm still pissed at him and it's going to take a few more days and a lot more groveling to make it up to me. Asshole.

After reading and listening to Gray's messages I see I have a message from Brett saying he will just meet me at my place to help me grab some things instead of me going to his since I told him I wasn't going to be having dinner with Gray. I knew he was open to compromising too, I always ask him if we can have dinner at my apartment instead of his but he usually says no because it's roomier at his place and I'm "supposed" to be moving in there, even though my place has all of one bedroom and a bathroom along with a small kitchen and living room, that's what I'd call roomy if you ask me. But after our talk this morning and him asking me to take a step back from Gray he seems to think he should give me something in return and that makes me extremely happy.

I knew from the beginning our relationship was one that could stand the test of time and one that would be able to bloom and grow alongside us. Oh lord listen to me sounding like a hippie talking about a blooming relationship, but whatever, I can't think of a better analogy right now because I'm too happy.

It makes me giddy to think how in the course of a day it seems like we have taken two steps forward in our relationship. I know I talk about how we may not be prefect for each other, but I really do think he can make me happy in life. It may not be everything I hoped and dreamed of, but it's also better than pathetically vying for my best friend like an idiot.

I walk into my apartment building and make my way upstairs. I live on the second floor of a small apartment building not far from downtown. It's what some would consider an old building, but to me it's perfect. I've always had a thing for older buildings, I love to just think of the stories it would tell if the walls could talk. I know that sounds creepy but that's not how I mean it, obviously. I may or may not be a hopeful romantic at heart and just thinking of the love stories these walls have seen and heard makes my heart happy.

Yeah, yeah I'm sure they've heard some not so romantic things and some stuff that's probably closer to rated R than PG but to me, romance is romance, and that includes the good and the bad parts. No relationship is perfect, never has been and never will be.

Some people say that there are relationships that exist where you feel like you're flying and could burst because you are so in love. I may not ever find that, but I do believe that what Brett and I have, even though it may not be the best love out there, I think it's still pretty good.

My romantic heart will probably never stop dreaming of the what ifs, but I am not the type of person to dwell on the past or the what ifs too much. If I was I don't think I would have ever gotten past my parent's deaths. It was hard enough the way it was losing my hero and one of my best friends in the same night, but at the same time I'm happy they went together. I honestly don't know how one of them would have survived without the other. I'm just happy they can still be together and never having to be apart. I honestly think that's what has gotten me through these past two years, is knowing that they are watching down on me together while holding each other close.

I walk up the step to my apartment with a smile on my face. As I get closer to my door I hear what sounds like muffled yelling. It isn't until I get right outside my door that I can hear Brett yelling at someone through the front door. He sounds furious, whoever he is talking to really must have pissed him off because I don't know the last time I've heard him this mad about anything.

I quietly open my front door and slowly make my way into my apartment trying my hardest not to make my presence known. "Are you kidding me", he bellows.

"I told you I needed the information by eight o'clock this morning in order to stick to my timeline. It is now creeping up on six. I gave you one job, Chris, to get me the information I needed by eight this morning and clearly that was too much to ask of you." I can see the vein on his neck trying to make its way out of his skin from where I'm hiding in the narrow doorway.

"What do you mean you can't find it? There's no way some old man could have done that good of a job of covering it up. I expect the information in my email by eight tomorrow morning or I will find someone who is capable of getting me what I want," he seethes as he slams his phone down on the counter thoroughly scaring me, causing me to jump back and hit the wall, which conveniently gives up my hiding place.

"Harmen is that you?" he asks from the living room as I could hear his footsteps bringing him closer to me.

"Yeah it's me," I call back trying to look as innocent as possible and not like I had just been loitering in the entryway eavesdropping on his conversation. I step into the living room and practically ran into him as he comes around the corner to meet me in the entryway. Startled, I reach out and grab his arms to steady myself and can instantly feel just how upset that phone call made him. He looks like he's barley containing his anger at this point.

"Why didn't you tell me you were home? Why were you hiding over here?" he asks with a scowl.

"I didn't want to interrupt you're call. You seemed upset and I didn't want to bother you, I'm sorry," I say while looking down at the happy

"Hello Sunshine" mat by the front door. I could tell he didn't care about my apology so I continued, "Whose Chris? You seem really upset by whatever he was saying. Are you okay?" I ask him while softly rubbing my hands up and down his arms in attempts to calm him down a little bit.

At the mention of this Chris fellow's name I can feel him go even more rigid under my hands if that's even possible. You'd probably suspect I just told him I kicked his dog or something terrible like that from the way he's reacting to the mention of this dude's name. I look up into his eyes and see what looks like hatred there, but that can't be right. I don't know who the guy he was talking to is, but he can't hate him. Brett isn't like that.

Besides his temper Brett is a loving guy who never has anything bad to say about anyone and gets along with everyone, well except for Grayson of course. But before I even get a chance to inspect that look in his eyes it's gone and back is the loving look I usually see directed at me. After taking a deep breath and removing himself from the hold I have on his arms he turns to walk back into the living room and looks at me over his shoulder with a smile. "I'm okay beautiful, he's just a new guy at the office who doesn't know what he's doing yet but he'll figure it out."

"Why were you so upset though, did he mess something up for you?" "He just forgot to get me something that I needed by this morning, but it's nothing for you to worry your pretty little head about, okay? It's just work, I don't want it to ruin our night."

With a small sigh of defeat, I know I won't get any more information out of him. "Okay, as long as you're okay," I say making my way into the kitchen to set my bag down on the table. I'm not sure if he says anything else or not because I'm walking and trying to listen when I see the gigantic bouquet of purple and white calla lilies resting in a stunning vintage blue vase on the kitchen table.

This day started off terribly by fighting with my best friend, but it seems to have turned around completely. Flowers are the way to my heart and I'm so surprised to see the bouquet sitting on the table because Brett has never gotten me flowers before, let alone my absolute favorite ones. I slowly walk up to them and reach out and pull a silky petal between my fingers. I don't even have to bend my head to smell them because they are already filling my entire apartment with their heavenly fragrance.

I slowly look up to find Brett standing on the other side of the table giving me one of his many smirks. "I can't believe you got me flowers Brett, let alone calla lilies. How did you know I loved them?" I asked him with a look on my face that told him he could take whatever he wanted from me as long as he kept getting me flowers.

At least I think that's what the look on my face shows. And honestly the boy could use me however he wanted and I wouldn't mind one bit as long as he keeps bringing me flowers. Yes, I'm a flower whore. What can I say, my mama raised me right.

"Lucky guess," his answer that tells me he knows what I'm thinking. I make my way around the table, stand up on my tiptoes and pressed a kiss to his cheek.

"Thank you, I mean seriously you have no idea how happy these make me."

"I'm glad, you know that's all I ever want is for you to be happy." Apparently Gray isn't the only one saying that today.

"Well I am, you make me very happy," I reply as I reach up to give him one more kiss on his cheek.

After grabbing a bottle of water from the fridge that's probably older than my deceased grandma, I make my way back over to the table where he is still standing looking at the flowers with a slight scowl. Once I get closer his head snaps up with a worried look taking over his gorgeous features. "Did you talk to Grayson today?" Oh so that's what the scowl is about. Shocker. Taking a deep breath, I meet his gaze.

"Yeah I did. He wasn't too happy about it but I told him he needs to respect our relationship." A slow grin spread across his face as he steps closer to me.

"You really said that?"

"Of course, why wouldn't I? You're my boyfriend and after what you said this morning it makes sense to me. I told him we needed to go out together less which really pissed him off, but I told him he can either support me and my relationship with you or he can leave me alone." I reached up and cupped his cheek with my hand and said in a hushed voice, "I want you to be happy and if that means me spending less time with Gray than I'll do it." His slow growing smile has now turned into a full-fledged grin.

He reaches up and pulls my hand off of his face and intertwines our fingers, "You make me so happy, Beautiful. Let's go to dinner so I can come back and show you just much I appreciate you," he practically purrs into my ear. You don't have to tell me twice. I lean back and try to give him my sexy smile, it probably makes me look like I'm constipated or relieving myself of some other sort of bodily fluid, but he doesn't seem to notice.

"Okay, let's go," I grin and pull him by his hand towards the door all too excited to get this night started.

We got home close to eleven after a night full of wining and dining. Brett was so attentive all night, it started when we arrived at the restaurant he held the door open for me as we walked in and he even opened the car door for me before that. Once we got up to the hostess stand and he gave the blonde bombshell manning the desk his name we were escorted back to our table right away.

It didn't sneak past me that the hostess kept looking over her shoulder and giving my boyfriend some pretty friendly eyes. I'm sure she's a great girl, when she's not making eyes at my boyfriend, but to my surprise Brett didn't even so much as look at her. It's not that I thought he would... okay I guess I thought he would, that's probably why it made me that much happier when he didn't. It reminded me of our first date at the small Italian restaurant with the waitress drooling into my soup over Brett, but he didn't notice her, even then.

After she shook her hips all the way to our table Brett pulled my chair out before we sat down, which lead to her huffing and puffing while making her way back to the front. Over dinner he called me beautiful more times than I could count and that really does a number for a girl's confidence if you ask me.

It's not that I thought I looked bad but I just never thought I could live up to his amazing modelesk looks. I mean come on, the man was pretty much straight out of a Hollister add and they probably wouldn't even let me into Hollister without a few heavy eye rolls as I stumble my way through the doors. He was pure man and muscles and pretty much everything else that could make a girl swoon just by looking at him.

Not me though, nope. If I'm being honest, most times my long dark hair gets stuck in my arm pits even when I put it up in a ponytail, but I just can't bring myself to cut it. And apparently that can turn some men away, who knew. I always wish my blue eyes could be a little bluer and my skin could be any shade other than pasty, but that's just how God made me so I guess I'll roll with it. I'll just go out and get a spray tan here and there to pretend I'm not basically albino. I also tend to think I look like a man, minus a penis. It's not that I'm hairy or anything, jeez I do shave... sometimes.

I definitely have an athletic build rather than a nice feminine figure, but I guess that's what made me able to kick the guys' asses in gym back in high school. But now that I'm older and with Brett I wish my boobs were maybe a little larger than pebbles and maybe I could get some hips while I was at it too.

So let's just say I barely fill out the gray sweater dress I'm wearing paired with some black booties. It's about as dressy as I get which is fine with me. Brett was looking absolutely gorgeous in a pair of dark jeans and a white button down rolled up to his elbows to show off his fit forearms. Let's just say he looked mighty fine sitting across from raggedy ol' me.

By the time we got home I was ready for some alone time with my incredible boyfriend. I just wanted to get my hands on him and I could tell he wanted to get his on me, even though I'm not sure why. I feel like this is how relationships are supposed to be, I can honestly say I think I have finally fallen in love with my boyfriend. Now if only my best friend could be happy for me.

CHAPTER 5

Grayson

I'm currently still standing outside of the small café while our audience from five minutes ago watch me through the windows like I'm some sort of wild animal. I don't get where she would have gone in the two minutes it took for me to follow her out the door. She may be fast but she's not that fast. Feeling defeated I make my way back to my car parked on the side of the street a way down.

Why do girls have to be so difficult? Okay, that's probably not the right thing to say – let me rephrase. Why does my best friend who is of the opposite sex have to be so difficult? I mean really, how can she not see that prick is trying to change her. No one is their right mind should ever try or want to change Harmen Brooks. She's what I would call a diamond in the rough, super cheesy I know. She's everything any guy could ever want rolled into a nice small package.

Don't get me wrong, she definitely has her

faults. Especially when she turns into Harm – the deadly dragon who lives and breathes fire and harm – hence the name. But more often than not, she is the type of girl that belongs in every guys' fantasy, even though I would personally pummel any guy whose fantasies star Harmen.

Once I close the door of my small two door sedan I reach into my pocket and to pull out my phone. I know she is going to ignore me if I call or text her, but I can't help it. She's my best friend and I hate when she is upset with me, even though I love to piss her off. I know it doesn't make any sense, but I don't care.

I pull up my messages and send her a quick apology. "*I'm sorry Har. I didn't mean to upset you... I just wanted to understand and for you to hear where I was coming from. I hope I'm still your best friend. Love you.*"

Every time we get into any kind of argument or disagreement I make sure to drop the best friend card. I want her to realize that I will always be her best friend and that she can trust that I won't be going anywhere, even if she tries to force me.

I would honestly do anything for the girl even if it means apologizing when all I am doing is trying to look out for her and I hope that after all of these years she knows that. She is the most important person in the world to me and I just want her to be happy and safe. I know she says she's happy with him, but I don't know that she's truly safe.

She may be physically safe but I don't know that she is emotionally. I don't know how to explain it, there's just something about that guy that rubs me the wrong way and always has. Maybe it's how it seems like he's constantly trying to change my best friend even though she is the most incredible person in the world just the way she is. I know she doesn't see it or notice that he's doing it, but I can see it and I don't like it. Not one bit.

After a couple more unanswered messages and calls I make the executive decision to show my friend just what she means to me. In a completely platonic way of course. No matter what Harmen says she is a complete sucker for flowers, specifically white and purple calla lilies. I honestly think she would have them in every room of her apartment if she could.

She's loved them since we were little and she attended one of my family's friend's weddings. The bride decided to go with a plum and ivory color scheme with the same colored calla lilies. At the dance my friend wanted to catch the bouquet just so cold take the flowers home with her. She ended up using her scrawny elbows to take out the girl to her right before she caught the flowers and that's how my best friend ended up catching the bouquet at ten years old. Great story, I know.

Let's just say the flowers had a spot of pride on her night stand for the next year until I could convince her to finally throw them away when I bought her new ones. Ever since then she has had a secret love for them so I know I can at least put a smile on her face if I get her some.

I make a pit stop at the small flower shop downtown to pick her up some flowers. The older lady who owns the shop, Mrs. Kelley, knows exactly what I'm there for when I walk in the door seeing as how I always get Harmen a bouquet when I've upset her. "Are you here to grovel again boy?" Mrs. Kelley asks with a knowing smile on her face.

"Yes ma'am, I sure am."

"What'd you do this time?" "Politely tried to tell her that her boyfriend is trying to change her and that she could do better than him," I say with a tight smile.

"And are you the guy she could do better with?" Ah this old lady knows more than I thought she did.

"You said it not me," I answer with a wink.

"Oh boy, you are trouble aren't you?" she asks while laughing at me.

"Some would probably claim so," I answer truthfully.

"Well, let me run in back and grab you what you came here for." After she leaves the room I peruse around looking at all of the little knick-knacks she has lining the shelves. My eyes get caught on a light blue vintage vase that reminds me of my best friends eyes. I knew she has to have it the second I see it.

I grab it off the shelf and bring it up to the counter as Mrs. Kelley comes from the backroom carrying a bouquet of white and purple calla lilies for my favorite girl.

"Looks like you found something else did you?" she asks with a pleasant smile.

"Yeah, she loves everything and anything that could be viewed as vintage or an antique. So why not try win her over a little more. Plus, if I'm being honest, they remind me of her eyes," I say feeling shy all of a sudden. I feel Mrs. Kelley lean over and give my hand a reassuring pat before turning to the cash register and ringing up the flowers and vase.

After the bill is settled I ask her if she could fill the vase with water and the flowers. She comes back out a couple minutes later and hands me the vase that is now spilling over the edges with my best friend's flowers.

"You know boy, one of these days you'll have to tell her how you really feel."

"I know, but today isn't that day, maybe someday. Thank you Mrs. Kelley," I say as I make my way towards the front door.

"Fine, maybe not today but one day soon. You owe that girl and yourself that much," she yells as I reached the door.

"I know Mrs. Kelley, I will. One day soon, I promise," I respond as I walked out the door and get back in my car.

On my way to Harmen's apartment I call

and message her a couple more times. Still no response, not that I'm surprised though. I leave her a message asking her if she was home, but of course I won't get an answer to that either. I know she has classes all day, but I'm guessing this has more to do with her ignoring me than being busy with class. I pull into a parking spot outside her building, grab the vase of flowers, and make my way inside.

Once I'm up on the second floor and making my way towards her apartment, I stop when I reach her door and hear what sounds like yelling coming from her apartment. I move closer to the door to try get a better listen to what's going on inside.

I'm about to raise my fist and knock her door but stop when I notice the yelling inside is coming from a man. It takes me a minute to recognize the voice as Brett's. It sounds like he's yelling at someone about some kind of information he needs, but I don't hear Harmen's voice so I'm not sure if she's home or not since I didn't see her car out front.

If he's yelling at my best friend this guy's got another thing coming. I decide to nip it in the butt and loudly knock on the door. I hear Brett's hushed voice telling someone to hold on. I knock again when he doesn't answer the door right away but stays quiet.

Why would he be yelling and not think about people hearing him? This guy must really be stupid. And more than that who is he talking to? I don't hear any other voices in the apartment so he must be on the phone, but why is he in Harmen's apartment without her there?

I give it one more shot and knock loudly on the door again to see if he will grow some balls and answer the damn door, but it doesn't surprise me when there's no answer. I decide to just leave the flowers outside the door and hope that she will see them when she gets home and know they're from me. I slowly make my way back downstairs still listening to see if I can hear Brett start talking again. After a couple seconds I hear nothing but silence coming from the coward inside my best friend's apartment.

It pisses me off that he's there without her. I know she told me a while ago that he mentioned he wanted her to move in with him, but it still bothers me that he's at her place without her being there. I don't even do that and I'm her best friend. And who was he yelling at? I know he works at some fancy pants lawyer office in town, but why would he be yelling at someone after hours. It's probably just something work related, but I can't shake the feeling that if he yells at his coworkers like that maybe he does it to Harmen too.

Once I get in to my car, I make the decision that I am going to do whatever it takes to keep my best friend happy and her heart safe, no matter the cost.

CHAPTER 6

Harmen

This week has been the longest Gray and I have gone without talking, but I still can't bring myself to answer any of his calls or messages. I don't know what it is about this fight that's harder for me to let go of but I just can't seem to get past it. Maybe it's because a small piece of me understands where Gray is coming from but the bigger part of me wants to and will stand by my relationship, until I have no other choice but to give it up.

It's Friday morning and I just got done with my early morning class. As I'm leaving the building I see Gray making his way towards me. It's not that I've been avoiding him this week, okay fine I've been avoiding him. I just want things to go back to how they were before he opened his big mouth and put his ginormous foot in my relationship. I wish he would have just continued to keep his thoughts to himself like he's been doing for the last two years apparently.

I contemplate taking off around the side of

the building or trying to hide in plain sight, but who am I kidding. I'm about as fast as a fat kid after Thanksgiving dinner, I'd never make it around the corner before he spotted me and I'd probably pass out along the way from the sudden exertion. Maybe my baggy sweatpants and sweatshirt that's two sizes too big will hide me from my traitorous friend.

No such luck, I've now taken too long contemplating my escape options that I didn't even notice he was now in front of me. Son of a bitch.

"Hey Har, I've been trying to talk to you all week but you keep ignoring and avoiding me every chance you get."

"Psh I wouldn't waste the energy avoiding you and I lost my phone that's why I haven't called or messaged you," I say with a tight smile just as my phone rings and decides to make its presence known. Ugh karma really is a bitch sometimes, isn't she?

After a dramatic eye roll for good effect I look up to see Gray looking at me with his stupid gorgeous face that's currently plastered with a smug smile. I hate smug smiles, especially from him since they show off his dimples. And I hate dimples... said no one ever. Ugh.

"What do you want Gray? Want to tell me how I'm wasting my time with my relationship or how I'm basically a puppet doing everything Brett wants. Oh wait, or did you just come to grovel so you can return to being my best friend?" I cross my arms over my chest and stand up straight in hopes of coming off as intimidating like I'm ready to fight if I have to.

"Relax Har, we aren't going to have a show down right here for everyone to see, you can put your arms down." Ugh I hate this boy and how well he knows me sometimes. "I just wanted to see you and say that I miss talking to my best friend," he says as a look of sadness crosses his face.

He knows I hate it when he's sad, I swear sometimes we know each other too well it kills me. "I miss you too, but that doesn't mean I just going to forget about everything you said to me."

"I know and I don't expect you to, I just wanted to see if you'd be willing to be around me long enough so we could talk and maybe get some coffee?"

How am I supposed to say no to him? Oh that's right I almost forgot, I can't. "Fine, let's go."

I start walking down the stairs toward the small coffee shop down the block. I don't have to look back at him to know he's following me. I also know he's got that damn smug smile of his back on his because he thinks he won, but he did not. Not even close.

Once we get inside the coffee shop I go up to the register and order my regular hot chocolate and chocolate chip muffin before Gray even gets to the counter. I know he will offer to pay and I don't want that right now. I'm still supposed to be mad at him and if he starts buying my food and acting like nothing happened I know I'll fall right back into our old routine and I can't let myself do that.

"If you wouldn't have run all the way here and walked like a normal civilized person I would have bought your stuff," he huffs while coming up behind me as I hand the lady my card to pay.

"Exactly, we aren't best friends right now so therefore I'm not going to let you buy me anything."

"Really? That's how you're going to play it? You're still that upset with me that you won't even call me your best friend anymore?"

"Yes. Right now I am that upset with you. Deal with it," I say with some added sass just because I know it pisses him off. And by the sound of his sigh behind me I know it had the exact effect I wanted it to.

I make my way to the booth in the back corner after the lady behind the counter hands me my hot chocolate and muffin. I've already dug into my muffin by the time Gray finally sits down.

"So what did you want to talk about?" I ask to try move this conversation along.

"Did you get my flowers?"

"What flowers?" I ask completely bewildered.

"The ones I left outside your apartment door last week after our fight," he says like I'm not completely lost.

I must look like I have no idea what he's talking about because after what feels like a couple years of staring at me he finally says, "You did get them right? I left them in a blue vintage vase that I thought you'd like."

Hold up. What? Is he seriously talking about the flowers Brett gave me? No. He wouldn't try to take credit for them. Is he doing this just to piss me off some more? No he wouldn't do that. Just thinking of him doing something like this just to piss me off makes me laugh. Pretty soon I can't hold back my laughter anymore and I'm basically rolling around on the floor of the coffee shop because I'm laughing so hard. I mean come on, Gray purposefully taking credit for something Brett gave me just to piss me off? It's laughable. Hence me doubled over laughing with tears streaming down my cheeks.

"Seriously Harmen, what're you laughing about?"

"That's a good one Gray, that's a really good one," I say wiping the tears off of my cheeks after finally getting my laughing fit under control.

"Harmen. Seriously what're you talking about? I picked them up because I know they're your favorites. When I was leaving I saw the vase and thought since I was an asshole earlier a nice vase for the flowers to sit in couldn't hurt my chances of getting you to forgive me. But if it was seriously that funny that I wanted to do something nice for you then I guess I won't anymore."

Woah. Is he seriously upset right now? No he can't be, it makes no sense.

"You're not serious right? Come on Gray, I know they weren't from you so you can stop messing with me," I say with a little laugh and wiping the last tear from my cheek. Apparently that wasn't the right thing to say. Now he just looks down right pissed. I'm pretty sure I can see some steam coming out of his ears like a tea pot.

"What do you mean you know they weren't from me?"

"How do I know? Well I know because they were sitting on my kitchen table when I got home from class. And on top of that my boyfriend was waiting for me at my place so he could take me out. He said he got me the flowers to make it up to me because I talked with you about cutting back on our time together that morning and he wanted to thank me for it. So how about you tell me why your saying they were from you when they clearly weren't."

I can honestly say I have never seen some much rage on a person's face as I do right now. I'm pretty sure I can feel the heat coming off of him because of how upset he is by my statement. Why is he so mad? Yeah, I'm not really sure. I'm as confused as he is apparently. Except, if anyone is upset it should be me. I mean, he's trying to take credit for something my boyfriend gave me for crying out loud.

"You've got to be shitting me," he says with a humorless laugh while rubbing a hand over his face. "That asshole boyfriend of yours gave them to you didn't he?"

"I just told you he did. Why does that make him an asshole? Because he cares about me enough to get me my favorite flowers? Really, Gray?"

"It makes him an asshole because I'm the one who bought them. I knew you were still pissed at me so I got you your favorites thinking that may help lessen the blow a little bit. I left them right outside your door because when I knocked you didn't answer. But now that I think about it, I did hear him inside your place yelling at someone. When I knocked he got quite like he didn't want me to know he was there even though I had already heard him," he says with a huff.

"Well I'm sorry to break it to you, but Brett wouldn't take credit for something he didn't do. So I'm not sure what kind of game you're playing at but I quit," I say standing up. I'm officially done with this conversation. And I'm officially done with my best friend who is trying to sabotage my relationship. "See ya later, Gray."

I don't make it very far before I feel him grab my arm and spin me around to face him right by the front door. "Har listen to me for a second. I don't know why he said they were from him but I promise I left them by your front door. I heard him yelling at someone when I got to the door and thought it was you so I started knocking and that's when he stopped talking. I figured you were there with him and you guys were fighting or something. I'm not trying to play a game; you know me better than that. Can you honestly say I would try to take credit from something your boyfriend did?"

I don't know what to believe. I honestly don't think my best friend would do something like that, but then I don't want to think of the possibility that my boyfriend of two years took credit for something Gray did for me. I feel like I'm being pulled in two completely different directions.

My heart wants to believe my best friend but my head is saying to believe my boyfriend. Why can't they just agree on one of them? That'd make this ten times easier on me. I want so bad to believe my amazing best friend, the guy I've loved most of my life, but for some reason I just can't.

"I'm sorry Gray. I don't know what to think at this point," I say as I turn and pull my arm out of his hold and walk out the door. As I get closer to my apartment I can't help but wonder how he even knew I got flowers in the first place.

CHAPTER 7

Grayson

What the hell just happened? Am I in an alternate universe? Oh, maybe I'm on one of those prank television shows and someone is going to jump out and yell "Gotcha!". I hope that's what this is otherwise I'm at a complete loss for what the hell just happened.

I was almost giddy, I know that makes me sound totally unmanly but trust me I'm a total man, when I saw Harmen standing outside of Berg Hall after her class. I know she saw me, but to my surprise she didn't run away when I started making my way toward her. I'm sure she was trying to plan her escape but just never got a chance to execute her plan by the time I made my way to her. I probably had a look of complete surprise on my face when she agreed to go to the coffee shop with me.

It's not that I thought she would ignore me forever, but I also know my best friend and she tends to shy away from talking about things that might make her uncomfortable or upset. Hence her ignoring me for almost a week because I pissed her off and she probably had this notion in her head that it'd be awkward to be around me after that. She just doesn't know that it's always hard and a little awkward for me to be around her when all I want to do is yell at anyone that looks at her or comes within ten feet of her that she's mine. Even though she is Brett's.

I figured that the flowers I left by her door would have gotten me out of the dog house for a little bit at least, but when I didn't hear from her I kind of gave up hope that they would. That's why I asked her to go get coffee with me, besides just missing her I wanted to know why she was so mad. I mean I get it, I was a complete ass with my approach the week before but I was just trying to look out for her, and maybe turn her off of Brett a little bit if I'm being honest.

But as luck would have it the prick hole decided to take credit for the flowers I got my girl. I mean seriously, I know he was a slimy snake for the beginning but taking credit for my flowers? Yeah that just pisses me off.

In the process he is pushing Har and I further apart and I know that's what he's been trying to do since the beginning, which is bullshit because she's my best friend and always will be. Even if she never again sees me as more than a friend I will always be in her life and will always do whatever it takes to keep her safe, especially from someone like Brett.

I just don't get what he is playing at besides trying to push us apart. I've never liked the guy, but lately there is just something I can't put my finger on that seems off about him. I remember the day Harmen and I were at the bookstore, which was the first day she met him. There was something is his eyes and the way he looked at her that gave me a strange feeling. At that point I didn't know I was head over tennis shoes in love with my best friend, but I still didn't like the way he was looking at her.

He almost looked at her as though she were a game of some sort. I know people say guys like to chase girls, but he wasn't looking at her like she was a challenge. He was almost looking at her like he already knew her, which makes no sense since neither of us had a clue who he was. The day they went on their first date was the same day her parents died in a car crash and he has been around ever since. He's like a nasty bug you just can't get rid of, always around and ugly as hell.

At this point I feel like I have to save face with Har or we are just going to push each other away with all this fighting. I think it's time I cinch 'em and go talk to the man of the hour myself. I should probably bring my fly swatter though, just in case he gets a little crazy and I need to squash him like the bug I know he is.

Seeing as how I don't have the spawn of Satan's phone number and I didn't really want to ask Harmen for it, so before I know it I find myself in the lobby of the law firm he works for. I ask the pretty petite blonde at the receptionist desk where I can find the one and only, Brett Worthington. She tells me his office is up on the fifth floor and to just take the elevator to the left.

I make my way over to the elevator and ride it up to the fifth floor. I figured his cubicle or small desk would be on one of the lower floors, not up on the same floor as the partners. But what do I know, obviously nothing.

When I step off the elevator, it feels like I walked straight into heaven, but I know it's really hell. The whole floor is open with a seating area in the middle, while different offices run around the perimeter of the floor.

Each office looks like it has floor to ceiling windows that make the whole floor light up. It makes me question why they waste the money on lights when there's so much natural light it's almost blinding. It also makes me question how a guy that's two years out of college, with no law school under his belt got a job here.

Harmen's mentioned a few times that Brett is considering going to law school probably once she graduates, but that he wants to give himself a couple years to see if it's a field he wants to be in long term. I mean sure, that's sensible. But at the same time, how the hell did he wind up here. Har told me that both of his parents died in a plane crash a few years ago so it's not like his daddy could have gotten him the job.

I look around at the different offices to see if I can spot him. I see his name on the outside of a door straight across from the bank of elevators. As I reach his door I see him working on his computer, I watch him for a couple seconds since he hasn't noticed me yet. I probably look creepy to anyone else on the floor, but I promise I'm not. I just want to take advantage before he notices me. Just by the looks of it, he seems more like a partner at the firm than a lousy assistant.

I knock lightly on his open door as he looks up and spots me. His face instantly drops when he sees me standing at his door, but he recovers quickly. He almost looked afraid to see me, like he was slightly panicked. I mean I know I'm an intimidating guy, but really?

"Hey Grayson. To what do I owe the pleasure?" Smug son of a bitch recovered pretty quickly from his look of terror.

Stepping into his office and looking around I say, "Nice office. I was hoping to talk to you quick. Sorry about just showing up, I hope that's okay? I don't have your number so I figured this would work."

"Sure, come in and have a seat." I sit down in the overpriced arm chair across from his desk. "As nice as this visit is, I'm hoping you won't be offended if I ask you to keep it short? I have some work I have to get done before a meeting I have in an hour."

"No that's just fine, I'll keep this short."

"Glad to hear it. What can I help you with then?"

"I just wanted to come and clear the air. I know Harmen is important to both of us, but I hope you know I will always be in her life. We've been best friends since we were little and I don't think that will be ending anytime soon."

"I understand where you're coming from, but I hope you get that I will be the most important man in her life. I don't plan on going anywhere anytime soon or ever if I can help it. Look," he says leaning forward and resting his crossed arms on the desk, "I know you're in love with my girlfriend. I get it, I am too obviously. But I hope you respect that I am her boyfriend and hopefully one day in the near future her fiancé and then husband, while you are and always will be just her friend. You missed your chance in high school and now it's time for you to move on," he said with a smug smile on his lips and he leans back in his chair like it's a throne.

This dick really thought I was here to try steal her away? Okay so maybe I want to, but that doesn't mean I'm going to. If I ever get to end up with Harmen I want it to be because she wants to be with me just as much as I want to be with her and I want her to realize that on her own. Not with me breathing down her neck, which I've always wanted to do but that's a topic for another time.

"I'm not here because I'm in love with my

best friend contrary to what you may believe. I actually came here to see if we could clear the air. I don't think either of us plans on leaving her life anytime soon, which means we will have to be able to be around each other without open disgust written on our faces. I'm not saying we need to be buddy-buddy because let's be honest, hell would probably freeze over before that were to ever happen. But for the sake of the girl stuck in the middle don't you think we can at least be civil?" Somehow my statement must have struck the wrong cord with him because now he looks down right menacing.

"Alright Grayson, let me frank. You and I will never be friends. Harmen is my girlfriend and yes she may be your friend, for now, but if I have anything to do with it you two won't be friends for much longer. She only has the need for one man in her life and that man is me. I know you'll probably leave here and call her as soon as you're out of the building. You'll tell her how I'm trying to force her to choose and how I'm trying to sabotage your lifelong friendship, but news flash, she won't believe you." The more this guy opens his mouth the more I want to kick him in his berries just for hell of it.

"Excuse me? Are you threatening to ruin my relationship with Harmen?"

"No Grayson, I would never threaten you or your relationship with my girlfriend. I think you will sabotage it all on your own, I mean how many fights have you guys had in the last week? I'd saying you're actually doing a great job of it already. Don't you think?" he asks with a smirk that tells me he really thinks he's going to win this. Well game on asshole. No one takes my girl away from me.

I'm seconds away from going full Tarzan on his ass and starting to pound on my chest to show him who the real man is. Just as I'm getting ready to open my mouth and tell him off he stands from his desk and starts walking towards the door.

"Where are you going? We're not done here," I say to his back as he reaches the door.

"Actually yes we are. I have a meeting to get to, but I'm glad you stopped by so we could clear the air." With that he turns and walks out the door leaving me sitting in his office wondering what the hell just happened. I seem to be wondering that a lot lately.

I know I need to tell Harmen what Brett said today, because I truly don't think I can hide it from her. No matter what he says I have faith that she'll believe me over him any day. Except today about the flowers I guess. But I try not to let that get into my head because I know it was a onetime thing. Just as I stand up out of the chair and turn towards the door Brett steps back in the doorway.

"Oh and Grayson, thanks for the flowers. She loved them." With a nasty smirk on his lips he turns and disappears into a conference room like he didn't just drop a nuclear bomb.

I'm pretty sure I continue to stand in his office for five minutes after he leaves with my jaw laying on the floor. I knew he took my flowers and gave them to Harmen himself, but I didn't think he'd actually come straight out and admit it. I'm not sure what kind of game he's playing at, but I know I'm going to do whatever I can to figure it out before it's too late. And maybe that means not telling Harmen everything I know until the end.

CHAPTER 8

Harmen

Later that week I get a text from Gray asking if I want to meet up for breakfast. Since I first brought up us not hanging out together as much we haven't gone to breakfast, which is huge seeing as how we used to go almost every morning. Over the last couple of weeks, I've realized just how much I miss spending time with my best friend. I don't really have any other friends besides Gray which means I've been spending all of my time with Brett. Don't get me wrong, I love it. But at the same time I miss my best friend.

It's especially hard to be away from someone you are used to seeing and talking to almost daily. When you become that attached to someone it's hard to put some distance between you, so I have to remind myself almost every day why I put that distance there in the first place.

You'd think after a day or so I would have moved on and been okay with the new way our relationship works especially since I was the one who changed it. But no matter how hard I try to forget, or how hard I try my best to focus on Brett, I can't get rid of the intense pain I have in my heart. I feel like I'm purposely pushing away a part of me and internally it's killing me, the worst part is at the end of the day I have no one to blame but myself. And knowing I'm hurting Gray in the process, yeah that's even worse.

I go to the corner café after telling Gray I'll meet him there and spot him sitting in our regular booth once I get inside. He doesn't see me yet, which gives me a chance to study him without him noticing, which also helps me seem like less of a creep.

His regular styled black hair looks disheveled, almost like his been repeatedly running his hands through it. I also notice his green eyes look almost dull compared to the brightness that's usually in them. As I get closer to the booth he looks up and spots me. I'm expecting to get a bright Grayson smile or a sexy smirk, but instead I am on the receiving end a tight lipped smile, which for some reason makes me pause. Looking at the hurt I see in his eyes makes me feel like a I have a ten-pound boulder sitting on my heart, slowly killing me from the inside out.

As I take a closer look at him I notice the dark circles that have a made a home under his eyes. It looks like he hasn't slept for days. I finish making my way to the booth and take a seat across from him on my side.

"Hi," I say with a tentative smile.

"Hey," he answers with a look on his face that tells me he's sad about something. "What's wrong? You seem sad about something."

"I've just missed you that's all," he says with the same sad smile. I reach across the table and grab one of him hands and give it a squeeze.

"Well, I've missed you too. I'm sorry for freaking out so much lately. I don't know what's wrong with me. I know you're just looking out for me like you always do, I just apparently didn't want to hear it."

"I probably could have done it differently, but I just want what's best for you and I don't think that's him. That's all."

Oh lord almighty and heavens above give me strength. I came here wanting to get my best friend back without any talk of Brett, but I'm starting to think that's not something I can just wish will happen.

"I appreciate that, but can we just leave it at what it is? I just want you to accept my relationship with Brett. I know you don't like him, but can you just pretend? For me?"

"Now that you mention it, that's why I wanted to have breakfast with you. I have something I want to talk to you about."

Why do I get a feeling I'm not going to like whatever it is that's causing him to be this upset? And on top of that I absolutely hate when someone says they want to talk about something. I mean come on, are you trying to give me a heart attack? My brain also jumps to the worst possibility first; it's just how I am I can't help it. Like maybe he hates me and doesn't want to see me anymore. Oh, or maybe he has a new girlfriend?

Wait, I thought he was still with that stripper chick? But now that I think about it I haven't seen her around for a while so maybe he cut her loose while he could. Oh wouldn't that be good news. Fingers crossed it's something like that. Focus Harmen, good Lord.

"Okay, what is it?"

"I went to see Brett at his office a couple days ago and talked to him."

"You what?" I ask with what I'm sure looks like a stunned look on my face. That was definitely not what I prepared to hear him say. I told you I always think of the bad things, never the good ones.

"I went to see him at his office because I didn't exactly have his number and I wanted to try clear the air."

"Seriously?" I think he's starting to get annoyed with me questioning him now. Oops. But, I mean come on. What's changed in the last two weeks that didn't in the last two years to make him put an effort in now? I'm just confused, that's all.

"Yes Harmen, seriously."

"Is that all you're going to tell me? That you went and tried to clear the air with my boyfriend? You're just going to leave me hanging?"

"No, I'll tell you what we talked about if you can calm down and stop asking questions long enough and for me to do so. Think you can handle that?" he asks with an amused expression on his face.

Laughing lightly, I leaned back in my chair and say, "Yeah I can do that. Sorry I just got confused and then I got excited. I thought it was going to be something terrible, you know how my brain works. This is what I've always wanted to happen and now that it is I just want to jump up and down saying praise Jesus. Okay now I'm rambling, I'm sorry. I'll be quiet."

He just laughs at me with a slight shake of his head and an adoring smile and mimics my move of leaning back in his chair and getting comfy.

"Okay so like I was saying, I went to his office in hopes to talk with him and clearing the air in hopes of finding common ground. Well, that common ground is you. We talked and just kind of got to know each other better since we've never done it before. We will never be buddy-buddy but we agreed to not show so much open disgust when we see each other from now on. And that's it."

"That's it?"

"Yes, Harmen that's it. Quite questioning me so much would you," he says with a big huff.

If I didn't know him so well I would believe him, but I know him better than he probably knows himself so I know he's not telling me something.

"That's a lie. There's something you're not telling me, Gray. I know it." He just sighs and rolls his eyes like it's this big inconvenience I know him so well.

"No there isn't. I'm telling you what happened. I thought you would be happy?"

"I am happy, Gray! I just feel like you aren't telling me something."

"Well, I'm telling you everything. I'm telling you that we agreed to be civil to each other from here on out. Isn't that what you wanted?"

"Of course that's what I want. I can't even tell you how much it means to me that you were willing to do that for me. But you promise you're not hiding anything from me? You know I can take it if you are right?"

"Yes Har, I promise. Nothing else happened. I just wanted to tell you so that we can go back to being friends. I miss seeing and talking to you all the time."

I go from not believing him, to believing every word that comes out of his mouth at the drop of a hat. Or actually I should say at the drop of my heart. That makes no sense, but oh well.

My heart and I are so happy right now I think we could both burst. If we did decide now was the moment to bust I know Gray would be there to tape both of us back together, just like he's always done no matter what. That's why I love him so much and always have. Well, not like I love

Brett, right? No. That kind of love ended in high school, I think.

Now I love him in a completely platonic way. Oh yeah super platonic, yup yup yup. I just don't stare into his bright green eyes for too long anymore or look at his dimples and chiseled jaw. Yeah he's basically my brother, and my heart feels the same way obviously.

I snap out of yet another internal monologue and find Gray staring at me. Oh lord have I been staring at him this whole time? I'm probably drooling. Let me check. Nope I'm good. I make a quick recovery and say, "I miss you too. These last couple weeks have been absolutely horrible not feeling like I could call or text you at any time. There were so many dumb little things that I wanted to talk to you about, but I didn't know if I could." Sadly, I look down at the table, upset with myself for putting a strain on our friendship in the first place.

"Of course you could have called or texted me at any point, Har. You should know by now that I always want to hear from you, even when we're fighting. You're my best friend."

"And you're mine. I know I didn't say it right away, but thank you for going and talking to Brett. I know you probably didn't want to, but it means so much to me that you did. I can't even begin to explain it," I say with a smile that's probably splitting my face in two as I speak.

"I just wanted to make you happy. That's all

I ever want to do." Ugh and then he says swoon worth shit like this that makes it hard for me to remember that I'm supposed to be looking at him like a brother.

Why couldn't he have loved me the way I loved him in high school? We could have avoided all of this and been happy together. What the hell Harmen? Stop thinking like that. It's in the past and Brett is your future.

Sometimes I swear I talk to myself more than I talk to other people, but who really needs a bunch of friends when you have your subconscious right? Not me that's who, I just need one. One very handsome swoon worthy best friend. Oh good Lord brain knock it off!

We talk for a little while longer, catching up on what we missed in the last couple weeks of awkward avoidance, then decide it's probably time to get going to class. Gray goes up to the counter to pay our bill while I grab my things and decide to wait for him by the front door. After he's done he comes up and opens the door for me to go out before him. Did I mention that he's a total gentleman too? Oh yeah, I have myself a very gentlemanly brother. Lucky me.

As I turn to ask him if he wants to walk to class I notice he looks more reserved than he did five minutes ago. His green eyes have gone back to the dull color they were when I first saw him this morning. I'm not sure what's going on with him, but as I open my mouth to ask him, he interrupts me. "Well thanks for meeting me for breakfast, but I have to get to work so I'll talk to you later."

"What do you mean you have to get to work? Where are you working? And why didn't I know you got a job?" He leans back on his heels and rubs the back of his neck with one of his hands as if he's unsure how to answer my question.

"Well I got the job I applied for at the Academic Records office on campus as a student worker and I started last week. I figured you were still mad at me for being an ass so I didn't think you'd really want to hear about it."

"Of course I would have wanted to hear about it," I say as I reach out to touch his arm only to have him take a step back. What the hell? He's never stepped away from my touch. I was just touching his hand in the diner not that long ago, what's changed since then?

I drop my hand before continuing, "Well I'm glad I know now and I'm happy for you."

"Thanks Har, but I better get going so I'm not late."

"Oh yeah, of course. I don't want you to be late. I'll talk to you later and thanks for breakfast," I say awkwardly while looking down at my feet on the sidewalk.

"No problem, thanks for meeting me. I'll talk to you later. Bye," he says with a small smile as he turns around and crosses the road to walk towards the main building on campus.

I stand there for a couple minutes and look

after him wondering what it is I missed. He has never shied away from my touch, it used to seem like he almost wanted me to touch him. I know there is something he isn't telling me, but I can't figure out if it's about Brett or something else. Either way, I know I need to find out.

CHAPTER 9

Grayson

I walk into the main building on campus feeling a little bad about breakfast with Harmen. I went into it knowing I needed to pull back a little bit, but I had a little more faith in my abilities to do it subtly than I apparently have. Anyone in a ten-foot radius could probably tell I was hiding something from her.

Ah hell and then out on the side walk when she touched my arm all I wanted to do was pull her into my chest and never let her go. Instead, I stuck to my stupid ass plan and pulled away. If my shifty face while telling her about talking with Brett didn't give away that I was hiding something, then pulling away from her touch certainly did.

I can't even blame her for thinking somethings wrong. Obviously I'm not very good at hiding my emotions, especially from her. And on top of that I've never in my life, pulled away from her touch. Since high school I usually try to do everything I can think of to get her to touch me, whether it's hug her or just stand to close to her so she has to brush up against me. I know I'm pathetic, sue me.

It's probably a good thing I never play poker or plan on being one of those scary ass detectives that participate in the good cop bad cop scheme, I'd screw that up in two seconds flat. That's a promise. I know I need to give her some space otherwise I'm opening myself up to a whole heap of questions and I just don't think I can handle that.

Not because I would cave or anything unmanly like that, but let's be honest I can't lie worth a shit. It's not like it's some skill I once had and lost it over time, no I've never been able to, just ask my mom. Don't get me wrong I've tried plenty of times over the years, but it wasn't until later I found out I practically squeak like a frickin' rubber duck when I try to lie. Which is a lie itself because I'm one hundred percent man and men don't squeak.

Anyways, long story short, I suck at lying and Harmen knows better than anyone when I'm trying to hide something so the best game plan from this point forward is to just keep my distance. Only until I figure out what I'm going to do to get rid of the trash and then I'll get my girl back. Yes. My girl. Mine. Dammit now I just sound like one of those birds from that Disney movie about the funny fish.

Once I walk into the office I make my way

to the back corner of the overly small room that's considered the Academic Records Office. I'm one of many student workers that help out in the office throughout the semester, but thankfully today I'm the only one so I get the pea sized desk all to myself. While the computer boots up I contemplate what to do.

Over the last couple days since I talked with Brett I've been battling with myself about how far I'm willing to go to get rid of him. It's not that I want to get rid of him per say, I know I've said it before but there is something off about the guy. It's just this feeling I get whenever he's around and I feel like as a best friend it's part of my job description to vet him before he gets to comfy around my girl.

I'm typically a guy who plays by the rules and doesn't abuse the trust other people give me, but I feel like the dirt bag is hiding something and I just want to find out what it is. Call me curious. I've been debating whether or not to look at his information we have at the records office from when he was still a student. I'm pretty sure just the idea of doing it and knowing how much trouble I'd be in if anyone found out is giving me hives. All I know is since the idea popped into my head a couple days ago I've been one itchy son of a bitch. And I can't open my mouth to try lie my way through it or Lord knows I'll start squeaking all over the place.

While mentally slapping myself, I have to

remind myself that I'm doing this to protect Harmen. Alright, I made the executive decision to have a peak at Mr. Model's file. Well that was easy. Mention Harmen and apparently my brain decides to break all kinds of laws. I just won't speak about it and then I hopefully won't blow it. I'm a man, I can do this.

I just have to keep reminding myself I'm doing this for Harmen, to keep her safe and happy. And also because I hate the guy and I'm a nosey son of a bitch, but if anyone asks I'll just leave that last part out. Thankfully it's slow today and its only Mrs. Anderson and me in the office so I just have to wait the old bat out. I figure once she goes to lunch and I'm left covering by myself that'll be the best time to break the law. With less witnesses and what not.

A couple hours later I notice Mrs. Anderson is packing up her stuff to take off for lunch, so it's now or never. "Have a good lunch, Mrs. Anderson," I say like the innocent law abiding student I'm trying to tell myself I am.

"Think you can hold the fort down while I'm gone, Mr. Beck?"

"Yes ma'am, don't worry about me," I say flashing her my winning smile hoping to get her out the door.

"Okay, then I'll see you when I get back in an hour," she says as she walks out the office door with a wave over her shoulder. As soon as she's out the door I talk a deep calming breathe, look over my shoulder to double check I'm alone and decide to get down to work.

I pull up Brett's old information in the student database to see what I can find. Nothing seems out of the ordinary right away, just a copy of his admission paper work and a copy of his ID photo. Ah, he's such a handsome son of a bitch. Ha! Not.

After I flip through a few more things I stop when I come to a completed transcript with a school logo I don't recognize on the top. I snap a quick picture, hoping I can figure out where it's from later. After looking through more things I see his transfer paperwork from a law school. What the hell.

That doesn't make any sense though, why would someone got to law school and then come back to a community college? Also, I know I'm not brilliant by any means but I'm pretty sure you need to have completed your under graduate degree in order to even start law school. Right? I flip a couple more pages over and go back to see that the transcript I spotted first looks like a finished transcript from a college in Los Angeles. Thoroughly confused, I flip back to the beginning of the pile and pull his admissions paperwork again to take a closer look.

I start to read over the paper and nothing looks out of place just like I thought before, until I get to his birthday. The birthday he listed says he would be three years older than he told Harmen he is. Why would someone lie about their age and say their 25 when they're really 28? I honestly think I'm getting a headache from how confused I am. Everything else seems to make sense until I see the emergency contact he filled in. By the name she seems to be a woman and the address he listed puts her somewhere is Los Angeles. This just keeps getting more and more strange.

I take a quick glance up at the clock and see that I've already been digging through this stuff for forty-five minutes. I snap a few pictures of the admissions paperwork and transcripts and put everything back where I found it before Mrs. Anderson returns from lunch.

After everything is back in order and put away, I sit down in my chair and can't stop my mind from running. Why would he lie about his age? And who the hell is the woman he listed as his emergency contact? He told Harmen from the start he has no family left, so is it a long lost relative? But if that's the case and he knows her name and address then she isn't very lost apparently. But they don't have the same last name so she'd have to be from his mom's side.

Maybe she's a family friend or even just a friend since he apparently has no one else. I mean, that's the only logical explanation I can come up with. Besides just the emergency contact, what the hell is up with the transcript from a school in Los Angeles and the partial law school transcript? Why would someone want to hide those kind of things and why would he come to a community college if he already has his undergraduate degree? I'll be honest; I wouldn't step foot back on this dingy college campus if I already had a degree and had been accepted to a law school.

I knew there was something off about the guy, but I never thought he was lying about things like this. But there's obviously got to be a reason why he'd keep these things from Harmen, right? I mean what possible reason would he have to lie to her, and to the whole school really. There's definitely something going on and I'm going to make sure I'm the one to figure it out. There isn't a chance in hell I am going to give him an opportunity to hurt my girl, even if I upset her in the process, I know she'll understand that I'm just trying to look out for her. At least once it's all said and done, I hope she will.

CHAPTER 10

Harmen

I walk home after my classes feeling like the whole day has passed in a haze. I don't even remember going to my classes, that's how preoccupied my mind has been since Gray left me standing outside the diner this morning feeling more confused than ever.

I can't get past the feeling that he's hiding something from me. Actually let me rephrase that, I know he's hiding something from me. I just can't figure out what it could be. I know things have been kind of strained between us lately, but the only thing we have always been is honest with each other. Our whole friendship has been built on always being honest with each other, even if it may hurt one or both of us.

Sometimes the truth hurts and I learned that the hard way when I tried to tell Grayson I loved him back in high school. He told me then and there that he didn't want to do anything that could ruin our friendship, because for him it was the most important thing in his life.

Looking back at it now, I should have known he wasn't interested in me like that and probably never would be, but the naïve high school girl I was couldn't see past how I was feeling and how much it hurt to be rejected by my best friend. Over the months that followed graduation I got over my love for him and it became easier for us to get back to how we used to be and now how we are. I've clearly moved on from the love I had for him in high school, I mean it's pretty obvious I'm over it.

In my brain I know he wouldn't lie to me, but I can't help the little pesky bitch that's just relentlessly pounding in the back of my head telling me he's hiding something. I keep seeing the look on his face when he was telling me about meeting up with Brett. It's like he was trying to convince both of us that's all it was. These are the thoughts that have been pestering me throughout the day and have now followed me all the way home.

I go to unlock the door of his, or should I say our, apartment and find that it's already open, which is strange for it being only a little after four. Usually I'm the first one home every day since Brett always works late, which is fine by me.

Thankfully I don't hear a serial killer rifling around our apartment as I walk through the front door, even though I probably wouldn't hear them until I saw them or they hit me over the head. That's just how my brain works, no use in trying to change it now.

As I walk further into the apartment the first thing I notice is the suit jacket Brett was wearing this morning laying over the arm of the couch in the living room. Maybe he is home? Wouldn't that be a nice surprise.

I set my bag and coat down, then cautiously make my way towards the kitchen where it sounds like someone is messing around with pans. I around the corner to see Brett bent over the stove trying, and I use the term trying very loosely since I've never seen him in the kitchen doing anything other than eating or drinking, but right now it looks like he might be trying to make something on the stove.

Did I wake up in an alternate universe this morning or something? Maybe I fell and hit my head and I can't remember? Oh, maybe I got hit by lightning, even though it hasn't stormed in weeks, maybe it struck me while I was walking to the diner this morning and I just didn't notice. You never know, it could've happened.

What else could possibly explain the strange way my best friend was acting this morning and that he seems to be keeping something from me and then I come home to find my boyfriend home early and not just that, but he's cooking in the kitchen. Cooking. Holy shit, that just doesn't happen.

I hesitantly step into the kitchen since I don't think he heard me come in and tentatively try to make my presence known without freaking him out. I know how much he hates it when he thinks I sneak up on him, and after the day I've had I don't really want to deal with that too.

Before I can chicken out I quietly say, "Hey, what're you doing home so early?" Once he hears my voice he slowly turns around and flashes me that insanely handsome smile that makes my insides shake with excitement every time he directs it at me. Even since that first day in the bookstore it makes me all flustered. I mean is it hot in here or is it just that smile? Phew.

"Hey, I didn't hear you come in," he says resting his hip on the counter while facing me.

"What're you doing home so early, is everything okay?" I ask with a little panic in my voice, I mean why else would he be home so early? Maybe someone died? Oh, no please don't say someone died.

"Did someone die?" I ask before I even realize I said it out loud. My damn mouth has a mind of it's our apparently.

"No Harmen, God no, nobody died, why is that the first thing that pops into that gorgeous head of yours," he says while slowly making his way over to me.

After taking a deep breath I look up at him and smile, "Ugh, you're right I'm sorry, I don't know why my brain went there. It's just so strange for you to be home this early and are you cooking?" I can't help but ask that with a little bit of humor in my voice after sniffing the air like a dog to confirm that he is in fact trying to cook something. I mean come on, the man never cooks how can I not find it kind of funny.

"Well yeah I was hoping to try make spaghetti before you came home as a surprise but I couldn't find the right pan and then I didn't know what to do with the jar of sauce. I tried to look it up on my phone but it was taking too long so I just put it in the first pot I found and turned it on. I figured what the hell, it shouldn't be that hard to heat up the sauce."

Ugh my ovaries are going to burst with how damn cute he is right now. He's always so sure of himself, it's a little strange to see him almost nervous about something. He's usually so serious about everything too, it's nice to finally see him let loose a little bit.

As I look at him and am about to say something I see smoke coming from over his head and I mean I know he's smoking hot, but I don't think he's literally smoking. I look around him to see the pot he put on the stove that must contain the sauce is currently smoking like it's trying to get high.

Before I can say anything else I sprint around him and pull the burnt sauce off the burning and turn it off while waving my hand over the pot to try clear some of the smoke that's gathered in the kitchen.

I can't help the laugh that leaves my throat

as I take in the burnt sauce and the look on his face that tells me he has no idea what happened. "Honey, please tell me you didn't put it on high and just leave it on there," I ask while laughing and shaking my head.

"Yeah, I wanted to try make it fast so I figured high was the way to go." He shrugs while looking a little embarrassed. Again, I'm not sure I've ever seen him look embarrassed. I really must have woken up this morning in an alternate universe.

Once the smoke has decided to calm itself down I walk over to him and wrap my arms around his middle and squeeze tight while looking up at him and smiling. "Well hot is okay if you make sure you're watching it, so next time just make sure to stir it and keep an eye on it. But I love you for trying."

"I love you too. I just wanted to try come home early for once and surprise you that's all, I'm sorry I couldn't do it."

"Hey, don't be sorry. It's the best surprise ever after the day I've had to find you home early." I reach up and give him a kiss on the cheek then untangle my arms from him and step back a little.

"I'm glad you're home because I wanted to ask you something if that's okay?" I ask hoping he'll be honest with me about his chat with Gray. Since I know Gray was lying to me earlier I might as well ask my boyfriend who hasn't lied to me about anything in our relationship. That much

I'm sure of.

"Sure, of course you can ask me anything," he says sweetly.

"Okay so, I met with Gray this morning for breakfast since I haven't seen him in a while and he brought up the fact that he stopped by your office a couple days ago. Is that true?"

I can see the second his demeanor changes and it's at the mention of Gray's name. I quickly continue before he can get too mad. "He mentioned that he stopped by your office and you two hashed everything out. It made me really happy to hear that, but I couldn't help feeling like he was hiding something. Did anything else happen while he was there?"

He takes a deep breath before he answers my question. "No not that I can remember. I'm not sure why he would be keeping something from you, but you know I'd never lie to you," he says with his charming smile.

I can't help but feel like there is something neither of them are telling me and it's really starting to piss me off. What would change to make my best friend keep something from me? He's never lied to me before so why would he decide to start now? It just doesn't make sense to me, I'd expect it from Brett, which probably says more about our relationship than I care to dig into right now, but not from Gray.

I feel a callused finger under my chin that makes me look up and see a strange look on Brett's face. I can't quite tell what it is but it looks like a mix between confusion and anger. Why would he be mad?

"Hey, it's going to be alright, I'm sure it's nothing. Okay?" I just nod with his finger still holding me chin up.

I know he sees the questions floating around in my eyes, but I do my best to mask them so he doesn't get too upset because let's be honest, that's the last thing I need to deal with right now.

He releases me chin softly, but stays in front of me and clears his throat. "So I have something I wanted to talk to you about, which is kind of the reason I came home a little early."

I looked up at him and noticed he almost seems nervous. Could this day get any stranger? Why would he be nervous, I can honestly say I don't think I've never seen him like this before. That realization puts a pit in my stomach thinking of all the possibilities of this talk he wants to have.

Is he going to dump me? Kick me out of the apartment and leave me homeless? Ugh, I'll have to move all my stuff back over to my tiny place and I really don't want to have to do that. No, he wouldn't do that, would he? Good lord almighty Harmen calm down and listen to what the man has to say before freaking out. Okay, deep breathes.

After taking a couple deep breaths I look up at him and say, "Okay, what's going on?"

"Nothing's going on, I just wanted to talk to you about something if that's okay?"

"Of course that's okay." I try to answer with a smile even though on the inside I'm dreading this conversation and currently trying to hide it.

He looks hesitant and he says, "So I've been thinking lately and I think some things need to change."

Oh shit here it comes, my head drops as he finishes. I knew it! He's going to kick my sorry ass out on the street and I'll have nowhere to go. I'll have to crawl back to my hole in the wall apartment while carrying my belongings on my back like a pack mule. And Grey claims I'm dramatic? Bull shit, I'm just realistic. I try my best to control the horror that's most likely written on my face and stay quiet hoping he will continue.

"I think we need a change of scenery."

My head snaps up so fast I'm pretty sure I just pulled something in my neck, but this is too exciting for me to care right now. "Change of scenery? Do you want to move or something?"

His shoulders shake a little as if he's laughing, now I'm just completely lost. "No Harmen, I don't want to move. I was more thinking along the lines of us taking a vacation. Getting out of here for a little bit to get away from everything and everyone just for a little while," he says while smiling sweetly.

"Wait, so you want to go on a trip? When? Where would we go?" He softly puts his hands on my shoulders.

"Breathe Harmen, it was just an idea. If you don't want to we don't have to, I just thought it could be good for us to get away for a little while and focus on each other instead of everything going on around us for a change."

Nodding I ask, "Okay, when would we go and where were you thinking?"

"I was thinking we could leave in a week and the destination will be a surprise. Do you trust me?" He asks with the most earnest looking on his face I've ever seen. He looks like he is waiting for me to either make or break his world. This is a lot of pressure. Deep breathes.

As confused as I am I can't help but realize that this is everything I've ever wanted from him. How could I say no to a trip with my boyfriend whose been there for me through some of the toughest times I've ever been through? I just can't do it and why would I even want to. But, do I trust him? I feel like that's the million-dollar question after the day I've had.

Before I even know what's happening I hear myself answering, "Yeah, I do." Again, my mouth has a mind of its own, but this time I'm happy with the response.

CHAPTER 11

Grayson

I can't help but reread the text I got from Harmen about an hour ago over and over again. I haven't replied because how do you replay to a message from the woman you're in love with who also happens to be your best friend, saying that her boyfriend said he's going to take her on a vacation in a week. I should be happy for her. Key word being should. Yet, I'm not.

I'm livid and keep feeling like I'm going throw up because of the information I found today at work and still haven't told her about. I've never lied to her before, or at least she doesn't think I have. Everything I've ever kept and still am keeping from her is for her benefit. At least, that's what I keep telling myself.

Harmen and I have said from the beginning of our friendship that we always wanted to be nothing but honest with each other our entire lives. To this day I have only lied to her once and I thought it was for the best interest of our friendship. When Harmen told me she had feelings for me in high school that were more than just friendly feelings, I froze.

For as long as I can remember I have been in love with my best friend. When we were younger I probably didn't fully understand the concept of love, but as we grew up and over the years there's never been a question in my mind and in my heart that I love my best friend with everything I am.

In high school I was too much of a pansy to do anything about it when she told me to my face how she felt about me. And it wasn't until Brett came into the picture that I realized just how much I really did love her, but by then it was too late.

I thought it would be best for our friendship, because I'd always told myself that I'd never be able to tell her how much I want her but that I was going to do everything in my power to make sure I always had her in my life one way or another. Even if it was just as a friend. I would deal with it, because the thought of not having that girl in my life one day makes me feel like my world wouldn't go on. So I told her what I thought would save our friendship at the time, that I thought we were better as friends and that I hoped it never changed.

To this day it's my biggest regret in life. I had her, the most amazing girl in the world, right at the tips of fingers but I was too much of a coward to reach out and grab her. Now I have to live with her being someone else's and I can tell you that is almost as painful as not having her in my life at all.

Unfortunately, it's a decision I made and one I will have to live with until the day comes where life gives me a second chance to reach out and grab her and I can promise, I will not miss it for a second time. Nothing is going to stop me from making sure she knows the real Brett, even if it breaks her heart. I just hope she'll let me be the one to put it back together afterwards.

That's why it is getting harder and harder for me to keep what I've found out about Brett from her. I just hopes she believes me when I finally do tell her. I tell myself once I have more information I will tell her everything, I just hope she doesn't hate me when that time comes.

"Focus Gray," I mutter quietly to bring myself back to the dilemma on hand. The damn text message.

How the hell am I supposed to respond to it? I hate lying to her but I don't want to tell her anything until I know more. So it looks like I'm just going to have to don the role of supportive best friend for the time being. Lucky me.

I don't get why he has the sudden need to go on a vacation? That's what confuses me most. Harmen's never even mentioned that they've talked about going on one or anything, so why now? Why so suddenly? The only thing I can think of is that my conversation with Brett the other day had more of an impact than I thought. Maybe he really does have something big he's hiding and this is his plan to run from it and keep it away from Harmen as long as he can.

Shitty for him, but I'm going to make sure I find out what it is he's hiding before they leave in a week. I'll make it my mission; she's not going anywhere with that lying piece of dirt without knowing the truth first if I have anything to do with it. And that's a promise. So time to figure out how to stop this before it's too late.

I decide it's probably best for now to play the ever supportive and encouraging best friend and text Harmen back, "*That sounds like it will be a lot of fun Har, I'm excited for you.*" There, done.

I pull the pictures I took of Brett's file up on my phone and flip through them. The age and law school transcript baffle me, but what really does me in is the emergency contact he has listed. All it has is her name, phone number and supposed address, but according to Harmen he has no living family so who could this woman be.

Sally Long, what a generic name, but then again she doesn't have the same last name as Brett, which is Worthington, so maybe she's a distant relative on his mom's side? I know I thought of all of this before, but I just can't get it out of my head. Whenever Harmen talks about Brett and his family she makes it seem like he has absolutely no one, distant or not.

I grab my laptop from my backpack that I left beside the couch and pull up a search engine. First things first, I need to know who this woman is. I type 'Sally Long' and her address into the search bar and pray something comes up. Not surprisingly there's a ton of Sally Long's in the Los Angeles area, but after a little more thorough research I find that there's only one at the current address listed. It might just be my lucky day after all, but it doesn't show any additional information like a spouse or anything else that might be helpful.

Against my better judgement I pick up my phone and dial the number written down on the sheet of paper I found in his file before I can talk myself out of it. I can't believe I'm doing this! I'm not the type of guy to meddle in other people's business, unless of course I think they may harm someone I care about. Then their business becomes my business no questions asked.

Before I can get too far into my head and hang up, I hear the phone connect on the other end. Holding my breath, I wait for someone to say something, anything. After a few hesitant seconds I hear the fragile voice of what sounds like a timid woman fill the deafening silence.

"Hello," she asks in a soft voice, almost like she was afraid to answer the phone.

After silently trying to clear my throat I say, "Hello, is this Sally Long?"

After another uncomfortable silence I get the answer I was hoping for. "Yes, this is she. W-who is this," she asks with a shaky breath.

"Hi ma'am, my name is Grayson Beck and I was wondering if I could ask you a couple questions about Brett Worthington," I ask cautiously. After I say his name I hear a quiet gasp on the other end of the phone.

After a long pause I ask, "Hello, Sally, are you there?"

What feels like a lifetime later, Sally finally speaks but in a voice so very different than the one she greeted me with when she first answered the phone. "Yes, I'm still here sorry about that I dropped the phone."

Umm, okay. It sounded like she had the phone the entire time, I mean I would've heard something other than silence if she had dropped it right? Instead of speaking softly and almost timidly like she did before, now she sounds like any middle aged woman on the phone. Her voice is strong and full of confidence, which is quite a contrast to the quiet woman I talked to not long ago.

Clearing my throat again I say, "Okay, so can I ask you a couple questions about Brett Worthington?"

With her newly strong voice she answers, "I'm sorry, I don't know who that it."

"You don't?" I ask hesitantly then continue, "He has you down as his emergency contact at Peskin University, so I guess I figured you would know him if he put you down as his contact."

"I'm sorry, but I don't now a Brett Worthington. Sorry I couldn't be of more help," she mutters hurriedly before hanging up.

After listening to the silence for too long I sit back on the couch and stare at the phone in my hand. She just hung up on me. What the ever living hell. I did not see the call ending that way. I feel like I talked with three different women in the duration of the three minutes I was actually on the phone with her. When she answered the phone she seemed almost scared to do so, but after I mentioned Brett's name she came back sounding like a completely different person.

She sounded so confident and like she was used to people asking her questions over the phone. Then not even a minute later after I mentioned Brett again she couldn't get off the phone quick enough. I feel like I have whiplash from talking to her for that short period of time. What the hell did I miss.

I know I'm not a detective or anything but I can't get rid of the feeling that she knew him and was scared to admit she did. Why would he have someone down as an emergency contact who was afraid to talk about him and not just that but deny knowing who he is? It just makes no sense to me. I have this feeling that she is hiding something big that will be able to put the pieces together for me.

If she isn't willing to talk to me over the phone maybe, I should just go to her and see her in person. Can I really do that, just show up at her front door and demand answers? No probably not demand, but I can try use some of my charm Har is always bitchin' about and see if I can get some answers out of her that way.

I stand up and march to my room with a different kind of determination than I had before. I start throwing things into a bag unsure of how long I will be in Los Angeles for. After zipping my bag, I take a deep breath and sit down on my bed. Resting my head in my hands and my elbows on my knees I can't stop the thoughts running through my mind. Am I really going to drive all the way to Los Angeles by myself and march up to this strange woman's door for answers? Answers that I don't even know she has. This so isn't like me. But I guess what they say is true, some people will do anything for love.

I can't just stand by and wait to see if something happens to Harmen or if Brett really is hiding something. I can't just sit by and let my best friend possibly be blindsided by something she may never see coming. And I know she won't see this coming when I do get a chance to tell her, but the idea that she may never actually find out about the things he may be hiding from her makes me sick. I couldn't live with myself if I just sat back and watched not just the woman I'm in love with, but my best friend be taken advantage of if there's even a small chance that I can do something to stop it.

With the decision made I stand up and walk out of my room with everything I need to go to Los Angeles and get answers for my best friend.

Let's just hope when I get there that I'm greeted with a different reaction than I was on the phone and that Brett doesn't pull anything while I'm gone. But I guess that's just a chance I'm going to have to take.

CHAPTER 12

Grayson

Last night when I got into Los Angeles it took me a couple hours to find a reasonably priced hotel room at such short notice. It appeared everyone wanted to charge me like I would be staying in the pent house even though most of them were run down and looked like they had seen their better days. Finally, I found an available room at an off brand version of a Super 8 that seemed to not be very far from the address I have for Sally.

I find myself waking up in the morning to a rumbling sound trying to figure out where I am, I reach over and grab my phone off the night stand to see I had just missed a call from Harmen. Scrolling through my phone I see that it wasn't her first attempt to reach me, nope. Actually it was her 11th. Ugh, this girl. She really is one of the most persistent and stubborn women I've ever had the pleasure of knowing. It's great for the most part, until I am trying to hide something from her or get away from her, in that case they are by far her worst qualities, well at least according to me.

Not only did she bombard me with phone calls all throughout the night but, I think she also literally tried to blow up my phone with text messages too. Ranging in anger from, "*Gray why aren't you texting me back?*"

To the last one, "*Grayson Allen Beck you answer your effin phone right now or so help me God!!!*"

There's the fire breathing dragon I know and love; I was starting to miss her. Oh and her love for cuss words kills me every time. You know she's pissed when she lets one drop, and yes, effin' is a cuss word in her book.

Clicking on one of the many missed calls I figured it'd be best I talk with her over the phone to try get her off my back or I know she'll just continue to pester me, which I really don't need right now.

After the first ring she picks up and sounds like nothing other than my favorite fire breathing dragon ready to tear me apart. "Where the hell have you been? Are you dead? You better be dead or close to dead or there is no other reason I can think of for you not to answer your damn phone Grayson," she yells at me through the phone.

"Hellooo Grayson! Answer me you dumbass, I know you're there!" Okay so maybe I didn't miss the fire breathing dragon after all.

Calmly, which I know will just piss her off more, I answer, "Hey Har, what're you doing?"

Just like I assumed, that really set her off. Opps. "What am I doing? WHAT AM I DOING? REALLY GRAYSON! I'm trying to find you're annoying ass since you decided to not answer any of my texts or phone calls. What the hell is wrong with you?"

My oh my, she must be in a nasty mood this morning with all the swear words she's throwing my way. I'm going to have to cover my ears pretty soon to keep them from bleeding due to all this profanity.

"I don't think anything's wrong with me, I was busy last night that's all."

"What do you mean you were busy last night? You're never too busy to answer my messages," she says with a huff then continues to berate me before I can get a word in. "Were you with a girl? Really Gray, you were too busy with a girl to at least let me know you weren't dead so I could stop losing my mind."

Huh, would you look at that. I wasn't sure what I was going to tell her I was doing because I know the second I told her I was down in Los Angeles she would go off the wall wondering what I was doing here and why. But looks like my lovely best friend just gave me the perfect excuse for my silence and she doesn't even know it.

"Okay yes, I'm sorry. I had a girl over last night and got a little distracted and left my phone in the kitchen all night so I didn't hear or see your messages till now, I'm sorry," I say with as much conviction as I can muster.

Then I hear her sigh in response and know it worked. Whenever I hear her sigh I know I've broken her down and gotten rid of the dragon, it's her tell.

"It's okay I get it, I'm sorry I freaked out so much I was just scared when you weren't answering your phone once you stopped answering my texts. I hope I didn't ruin your date," she says sarcastically.

"No you didn't ruin anything, you never do. Sorry I didn't respond or answer my phone sooner; I hate making you worry."

"I know you do, but it's okay you know I forgive you. On a different note, now that I know you aren't dead on the side of the road somewhere, we should go eat at the diner today."

Shit, I knew she wasn't going to make this easy for me. Let's see if she buys my bullshit again. "I can't today, and I probably won't be able to for a few days, I'm sorry. I have a ton of homework to catch up on and then I have to work on top of that. But soon okay?"

After a long pause she says, "Okay, fine. But promise me we will soon? Because I miss my best friend."

Son of a bitch, she wrecks my heart whenever she says that. Not only because I don't want to just be her best friend, but also because I miss her too. And sadly I have been constantly missing her for the last two years.

"Okay, I promise," I answer her honestly.

"Good and there's no backing out on a promise."

"Yes Har, I know. But I need to get going so I can get started on some homework, okay?"

"Okay, fine. Have fun and text me back if I text you. Love you Gray."

A big ass smile spreads across my face, splitting it in two when I answer, "Love you too Har."

With one last "Bye" she hangs up.

I fall back onto the stiff nasty mattress that will unfortunately be my bed for the next couple of nights, or at least until I get all the information I can on what's going on with that atrocious man. I absolutely despise myself for lying to her. Unfortunately, I have to just keep telling myself it's for the best and once I can get all of this figured out I can make my move and hopefully have her as mine once this is all over.

I know there's going to come a point in time where I will either need to make a move or move on. I'm just hoping by getting Brett out of the picture I can make my move and finally have what I've always been too scared to allow myself to have. Her. First I just need to find out what's going on with Brett and hope that I don't lose her in the process.

I pull into a rundown neighborhood later that afternoon. Based on the address Brett had written down on his form at the college, this is where Sally Long lives. I pull up across the street from a trailer home that looks like it's seen it's better days. I get the feeling that no one in this part of town has any kind of money, and what they do have they choose to spend on other activities.

I don't dare get out yet just in case someone is watching me. Okay fine, maybe I'm a little nervous to actually get out and walk up to her front door. I've never done anything like this before, obviously, but I just don't know how she will respond once she puts together that I'm the one who called her. If she was standoffish towards me over the phone, I'm more than a little nervous to see how she actually reacts to me in person.

I just have to keep reminding myself why I'm doing this, that's all that matters at this point. I don't know this woman and she doesn't know me, but I want to find out everything I can about how she knows Brett, no matter what. I can't leave here empty handed.

With hesitant steps I get out of my car and walk across the cracked street and up her front steps. Each one creaks and sways as I put my weight on it. I very well might end up falling through and breaking my neck and this will have all been for nothing. Before I can let myself get too carried away with all the what-ifs, I lift my fist and softly knock on the door.

CHAPTER 13

Harmen

I fall down onto the couch like a drama queen, but who wouldn't when their best friend hadn't been answering their phone or text messages all night long. I'm not crazy, he is. He doesn't seem to understand what it does to me when he just decides not to answer me like that.

It takes me back to the moment I found out about my parents. I know it's not the same thing and very unlikely that anything actually happened to him, but I just can't stop my brain from going there and he damn well knows it. So screw him for doing that to me. Now I just sound like a whiney little kid, but hell if I care.

After their deaths I attached myself the Gray. I depended on him for a lot of things which was never fair of me to do, but there was no one I trusted more than him. I knew he would never leave me unless he was taken from me, just like my parents. Yes, in hindsight it was probably unhealthy just how much I depended on him, but at the time it felt like he was all I had left.

He still had his mom and dad who loved him dearly, but it was always just us two. Mr. and Mrs. Beck both tried to comfort me after my parents' deaths, but I just couldn't allow myself to let them get too close to me without feeling like I was betraying my parents. I know my parents never would have viewed it that way, but I couldn't help my mind from going there. My brain just kept telling me it was just too soon.

After they helped me sell my parents' home and get all of their finances together I started to separate myself from them more and more. The further I got into my freshmen year at Peskin University, I found it easier to separate myself from them and focus more on Gray and Brett, I know they just wanted to help, but all I needed was Gray.

We did everything together, all the time. My freshman year I would stay with him or he would stay with me so I'd never be alone. As I got closer to Brett, it happened less and less, but it still was something we did whenever we would get lonely or one of us was in need of our best friend. He was and really still is my other half. That's why it's so difficult for me to let him go or not see him, even for just a day. I feel like I'm losing the part of myself that has always belonged to him, and probably always will.

After my parents died Gray obviously became the most important person in my life, and I believe he always will be. Okay well, I guess Brett should be, but if I'm being honest with myself I would always chose Gray over him. Even if I have tried to push him away for Brett's benefit, I was only lying to myself about being able to do it.

Maybe that says something about how I view our relationship and just how committed I really am to Brett, but I'll dig into that a different day. For now, I want to just relax and calm my mind down after my dumbass best friend refused to answer me, which inevitably led to me to thinking the worst possible things all night long. Shocker, I know.

It doesn't surprise me that he was with a girl and that was his reason for the silence, but that doesn't mean it doesn't bother me. If I force myself to be honest, I know there's a reason I get so annoyed and this feeling of dread in the pit of my stomach and a pang in my heart whenever I hear Gray talk about another girl. But I always talk myself out of it and stop my mind from focusing on it. I mean I have a boyfriend who I'm supposed to be in love with, why would I get jealous over my best friend being with another girl? Right?

Ugh, it's too early to be thinking about all these feelings. Just like every other day, I tell myself I'll come back to them at a later time. Even though it never happens. Oh well, it's the thought that counts. I'll let myself go there one day, but today isn't that day. I'm a really great procrastinator when I want to be. It's kind of a hidden talent of mine.

I sit up on the couch after hearing Brett walk into the room and say, "Good morning." If looks could kill, I think I'd be a goner right now. I silently read over his body language, which I've become very familiar with over the last two years. He's wearing pajama bottoms and a plain white tee, his feet are bare and it looks like he just woke up.

What could he be so mad about? Did a dream piss him off or did he just fall out of bed and hit his head or something? Oh, or maybe he pissed himself in his sleep, but I don't see a wet spot on his pants so that can't be it. Unless he changed them already? Makes no sense to me.

As he comes closer I can see the tension in his shoulders, his arms are straight down by his sides and he keeps flexing and unflexing his hands like he's trying to hold himself back. His number one tell of a bad mood is his jaw, he clenches it whenever he's upset about something and it's the easiest thing to spot. Looking at him right now, fist clenched, shoulders tense, and jaw ticking it looks like something has really pissed him off this morning.

I wouldn't say I'm afraid of my boyfriend, I'm just cautious of his moods. He has a pretty nasty temper, but doesn't everyone? Over the years I've learned how to defuse him if it calls for it. Usually all it takes is me just letting him get whatever it is that's bothering him off his chest and promising to do better and his mood will lighten. I know that probably sounds manipulative of him, but it's just how he is and it's the easiest way to handle his anger. So I just listen and try to be better so it doesn't happen again.

Slowly I get up from the couch and walk over to where he's standing, just outside the kitchen. Taking a shaky breath, I compose myself and get ready for the mouthful of words I'm about to hear.

I'm about the speak up to try defuse the situation when he asks, "Who were you talking to on the phone?" I feel my brows furrow in confusion.

Is that why he's pissed? Did I wake him up by talking too loud on the phone?

"I was talking to Grayson. Why what's wrong? You seem upset," I say timidly. My answer seems to do nothing to relieve his mood.

"What were you talking to him about?" he asks obviously still pissed.

"I called him a bunch last night and sent him a lot of texts because he wasn't answering me after I told him about our trip...," before I can finish my sentence he grabs my arm and pushes me against the nearest wall. Towering over me I have never seen so much hate in one person's eyes.

Before I can speak his grip on my arm tightens causing me to flinch in pain. "Why the fuck did you tell him about our trip? It has nothing to do with him," he roars in my face causing me to finch again. I've never seen him so mad before and I can feel myself starting to shake from fear. I don't think he'd hit me, but then again he's never grabbed me like this before either.

As calmly as I can, to try hide my shakiness, I looked at him and say, "He's my best friend and we tell each other everything. I was also so excited about the surprise that I needed to tell someone and he was the first person I thought of, I'm sorry."

Barely loosening his hold, he looks down at me and says, "Well it's not okay. He doesn't need to know everything we do all the time. You don't see me running around telling someone else everything about us do you? Do you!"

"N-no I'm sorry, I didn't think it was a big deal," I say with a shaky voice.

"Well it is a big deal, so listen to me when I tell you that you aren't going to do it again." His grip tightens on my arm again as he pushes himself even closer to me and says, "From now on you will not tell him anything unless I say it's okay, do you understand? Oh and before I forget, never fucking say "I love you" to him again. Got it?"

Why was he being like this? I thought we had gotten past this. Even though I said before he would never hurt me, I am starting to become more afraid of him every time he tightens the hold he had on my arm. He's never been this upset with me before and it's not like he hasn't heard me tell Gray I love him before. So why now? What's changed? That really seems to be the main question running through my brain lately.

Almost forgetting where I am, I snap back to reality at the sound of his hand hitting the wall right beside my head causing my eyes to snap back to his as he screams at me again. "Do you understand Harmen? It's a simple yes or no question. Answer me damnit!"

Trying to sound as confident as possible and without shaking I say, "Yes, yes I understand Brett. Can you please let me go? You're hurting my arm."

As if just now realizing how tight he's been holding my arm, he shakes his head and drops both of his arms to his side and takes a couple steps back from me. He rubs both his hands over his face before looking at me with a worried expression.

"Shit, I'm sorry. I didn't mean to hurt you. Are you okay?"

"Yeah, I'm okay, sorry I upset you," I say weakly.

"It's fine, you just know I get upset when you share our business with people."

He left out the part about how he hates when I share our business with people, especially Gray. I've never really understood why he seems to dislike Grayson so much, I mean I get that he doesn't always want me sharing our personal business with people, but he's never seemed to like Gray.

This is the first time he's told me not to tell him something. I just don't see the big deal about it, but then again I've learned over the years not to question him. It seems to be better for everyone, especially me, if I just listen to him right away instead of fighting him on everything. I know it's hurt mine and Gray's friendship, but I also know that he will always be there no matter what and I will continue to tell him things, apparently just not everything like I'd like to do. Or at least I won't tell Brett about it if I do.

I never wanted any part of our relationship to be based on lies, but if this is the response I'm going to get when I do tell him something he doesn't like, I don't think I want to do it anymore. Sometimes I wish it were all just simpler, that I didn't feel like I had to walk on egg shells around my boyfriend because I am scared of setting him off. I shouldn't have to live like that.

Looking back up towards his face, I can see that most of the fire has left his eyes. Even though there's still some lingering there, it seems like he's trying to push the rest away.

"I know, and like I said before I'm sorry. I won't talk to him or anyone else about our relationship again," I say hoping to get the last part of fire to dissipate from his eyes.

"Thank you babe. That's all I ask." He leans down to kiss my cheek and it takes everything in me not to flinch from his nearness. He gives me one last look at his eyes that no longer hold any homicidal flames in them then leaves the room. Crisis averted.

Once he's out of the room I slump back against the wall and let myself silently fall to the floor. Sitting on the floor of our apartment I finally feel like I can take my first full breath since yesterday. As much as I know it's probably best that I do what Brett says, I hate feeling like he's able to control everything I do and who I talk to.

I never wanted a relationship like that and I know my parents would be disappointed if they were here to see it. I just can't let a man change anything about me, especially who I talk to and who I interact with. That's not what I want for my life, so I'm going to do whatever I can to walk the line safely while making sure I don't lose any part of who I am while I'm at it.

The more I think about it, the more I start to this it's probably my fault. I suppose I shouldn't be telling another man "I love you", even if it is Gray. The only problem is that I do love him, I can't help it.

No, I can't let myself think things like this. This is exactly what I'm meaning by letting a guy change me. It isn't my fault, I know that. So then why am I so quick to make myself responsible for his actions? It isn't my fault he almost hit me and probably left a bruise on my arm, it's his.

I think I'm starting to lose my mind, not that I'm surprised, I always knew this say would come. I just thought I'd be in my 80s and in a nursing home with Gray when it actually happened, but apparently not.

Right now I'm just mentally and emotionally exhausted. I just woke up and I feel like going back to bed and pulling the covers over my head is the best thing to do. I need a do-over of this day and it isn't even noon yet. Lord help me.

CHAPTER 14

Grayson

Taking a deep breath, I raise my fist and knock on the rundown and splintered door in front of me. I have to tell myself to be patient to stop from pounding on the door and demanding answers, but I know that's not going to do me any good. So I patiently stand and wait, and stand and wait some more.

After a couple minutes of not hearing anything, not even the creak of a floor board from inside I decide to knock again, only a little harder this time.

"Maybe she didn't hear me," I mutter to myself. When I still don't hear anything I look around to make sure no one is watching me before I try to look in the window at the top of the door. I don't need someone calling the police on me for being a creep on an old lady's front step.

Reaching up I look inside and see nothing but darkness. It looks like all the lights are shut off and there's no sign that anyone might be home.

From the looks of the inside, it's in just as bad of shape as the outside. I sit back on my heels and look around. From the outside and even just the neighborhood the house sits in you can tell this is the run down part of the city, or at least one of them. It's nothing but blocks and blocks or run down trailer homes.

Each one looks like it's seen it's better days. Some have missing steps or fences that have fallen over from lack of care; some have boards on the roofs and windows, which I'm assuming is because they can't afford to replace the existing ones. The roads and sidewalks are over run by weeds, it seems that the city and even the residents don't care what it looks like.

On the outside Sally's house looks like it's been in a fight with a storm or two and the storm won. Yellow siding is falling from the exterior walls and it looks like some has already found its sanctuary on the ground. The brown shingles are starting to peel themselves off the roof like they are so repulsed by the home that they no longer want to be there. I can honestly say I don't blame them. Even some of the windows are boarded up and it looks like the steps I'm standing on are barely holding me up.

I reach up to try take a peek at the inside again to see how it compares to the outside. By looking through the small window at the top of the door I can't see much more than the kitchen and what looks like the living room. From what I can see, it looks like it hasn't been taken care of, pretty much the exact same as the outside.

Like I noticed before, no lights seem to be on and it looks like no one is home. Looking around at the mess inside, I notice food sitting on the table along with a coffee cup filled with some type of drink. It looks like it's been partially eaten, but that's as far as someone got.

Maybe someone took her? Maybe they came into her house when she was eating her breakfast and snatched her. What the hell. I'm starting to think like Harmen now and that's not a good thing. Honestly that's the last thing I need to do right now. I don't need to be jumping to conclusions and the worst case scenario just like she always does.

Resting back on heels again and lightly shaking my head at my absurd thoughts, I turn and look around and the neighborhood to see if anyone is watching me or see if anyone seems like they may know Sally. I'm not sure what I'm hoping for, preferably someone standing on the side walk with a big sign that says "I know Sally Long" would be helpful at this point. But I highly doubt I'm going to be that lucky today.

Walking down the steps toward my car I notice an older man standing outside the trailer next to Sally's watching me. Without thinking about any repercussions that could come my way or really about what I'm doing, I walk towards the stranger who's still watching me.

My parents always told me growing up to never approach strangers. You know the saying "stranger danger", yeah well my parents really tried to make sure I never forgot it. I'd say they did a pretty good job, up until now. I feel like I have no other option at this point so I guess I'm going to just forget that for today.

As I approach the man I take in his rugged appearance, long blonde hair that looks like it hasn't been washed in months, and baggy torn up clothes that make me wonder how long he's been wearing them. I have a feeling this is what most people in this area look like, unfortunately.

I can see the hesitation in his eyes as I walk up to him, I'm sure he doesn't know what I'm doing in a place like this and frankly I'm not so sure myself. I come to a stop in front of the man and try to come off as friendly as possible so I don't scare him away before I know if he can help me.

"Hi there, my name is Grayson and I'm a friend of your neighbor's, Sally Long, do you know where she might be today?" I ask the man. That made me sound non creeperish, right?

"How do I know you're one of Sally's friends and that you're not here to take her away?" he asks nervously.

I knew it, I knew someone snatched her! Holy shit, relax Gray and listen to the man before he kicks you off his property for strange behavior.

"I talked with her yesterday and told her I

would be coming down so I figured she would be at home. Why would you think I'd be here to take her away?" I ask confused.

"Cause the last time a man that looked like you that showed up here he threatened to take her away and hide her if she was bad."

What the hell is this guy talking about? I'm even more confused now than I was when I came here, which is just what I need. I put both my hands up to try help him calm down and see that I'm a friend of hers and that's all. Even though that's a lie, he doesn't need to know that.

"I'm not here to take anyone, like I said, I'm a friend of Sally's and was just hoping to talk with her. I was hoping since you're her neighbor you might know if she was home today. That's all, I'm sorry if I upset you," I say as calmly as I can. This guy already seems like he's on the edge of freaking out, no use in me pushing him over the edge.

"Okay, sorry I didn't mean to be mean, but that other guy that came by last week was about your age and came in here all dressed up in his suit and I couldn't help but over hear him yelling at Miss Sally that he would take her away if she didn't do what he said. I just didn't want to get her in trouble if you were with him," the man says with a long sigh and looks past me towards Sally's home.

I follow his gaze over my shoulder and notice a blind is being held back, as if someone is trying to move it to see outside. As quickly as I saw it, it snaps back to where it was before and looks as though no one had ever touched it. My eyes must be playing ticks on me at this point, unless she is home and is just hiding.

"No, I'm not sure who you're talking about exactly, but I'm definitely not with him or associated with him at all. I just came to talk with Sally for a little bit, do you know if she's home?"

"I thought so, but maybe she left for a while. Did you try knocking?" he asks.

"Yes sir, I tried knocking a couple of times, but it didn't seem like anyone was home."

"Well then she must have left for a little bit without me noticing. Maybe come back tomorrow and try again," the old man offered up.

"I'll do that. Thank you for your help sir. I'll come back in the morning and hopefully catch her. Thanks again," I say as I start walking back to my car across the street. I wave at the old man over my shoulder just before getting into the car.

Once I'm safely back in my car I start it up and head back towards the hotel. I can't help but wonder who the man was referring to when he talked about the younger guy in a suit who came and talked with Sally. I don't know much about her, but why would someone threaten a poor woman by saying they would take her away. Just seems odd to me I guess, but then again not a lot of things makes sense to me these days.

Once I get back to my room, I take a shower to clean up and end up lying in bed for the rest of the night. I guess I'll be going back to Sally's tomorrow, I just hope she's there and will talk to me even if it's only for five minutes. I just want to know who she is to Brett, is she an aunt, a second cousin, a long lost relative that he doesn't talk about much.

Who is she? And why did he have her listed as an emergency contact? I always had my parents down as my contact, while at school, someone who will drop everything and be there to help me if something goes wrong. So who is she in Brett's life that she would do the same and why hasn't he ever mention her to Harmen? That's the real kicker.

I reach over and grab my phone off the nightstand and decide to check it since I haven't all day and see that the only notifications I have are a couple text messages from Harmen, asking what I'm doing and when we can go to the diner next. Looks like they are from throughout the day, but unless I want a repeat of this morning I figure I better let the girl know what's going on or who the hell knows what she'll do. And the last thing I need is her calling me demanding answers about where I am and what I'm doing, when I don't know everything yet.

I decide to send her a quick message letting her know I was busy all day with homework and wasn't able to get to my phone much, and also that hopefully soon I'll have time to go to the diner. I hope it's enough to satisfy her, until I can get this whole mess figured out and tell her what's really going on with that slimy boyfriend of hers. Well if I can get to the bottom of it that is.

As I toss and turn all night I just keep having to remind myself why I'm here in this nasty run-down hotel room, on this lumpy ass bed. I would do this and so much worse just to make sure my best friend is safe and happy. I know she pretends to be happy, but I can see it in her eyes that she is trying to convince herself she is. I don't know that she actually is happy, from what I've seen and the Harmen I know, she's hiding something and I'm pretty sure it's something to do with Brett.

Lately I've noticed that she's a little more skittish, which I don't like or even understand, and she doesn't talk about him as much as she used to, but that part is okay with me. I keep telling myself that I'm doing this for the sake of my best friend and for the girl I love more than anyone or anything else. No matter what I find out or how long it takes, I'm making it my mission to ensure she is happy and safe in life, even if in the end it isn't with me. Once my brain calms down enough, I finally fall asleep and dream of what my life could be like if I am lucky enough to end up with the only woman I've ever loved.

CHAPTER 15

Grayson

After waking up and getting ready for the day I head out to my car and make my way back to Sally's house to see if she's home and up for a chat on this fine Los Angeles morning. As I pull up outside her trailer home and park across the street, I look around to see if anyone is out and about. The neighborhood seems to be deadly quiet, which doesn't help me at all.

I also notice that the man I talked with yesterday, whose name I never asked for, is not outside either. I'm not sure if I expected him to just be sitting outside waiting for me or what, but I find myself oddly disappointed he isn't outside waiting for me. I really could have asked him some more questions, especially if she doesn't answer her door again.

I look back at Sally's to see if I can see anyone in the windows watching me, but everything seems to be still. Nothing looks different or out of place since I was here yesterday, so maybe she never came home or she never left. I'm kind of hoping my brain isn't playing tricks on me when I swear I saw that blind move yesterday, but so far it seems like I was probably just seeing things.

I get out of my car and walk across the street and up her creaky front steps. Before I knock I try to listen and see if I can hear anything coming from inside, which ends up being a total bust. Either she really isn't home or she's hiding and doesn't want me to know she's home, which based on the warm welcome I got from our phone call a couple days ago it's probably the later of the two options.

Since I don't hear anything going on inside, I decide to knock just for the hell of it. Maybe I can catch her off guard and wake her up. Good Lord I'm a horrible person for hoping to wake her up. I doubt it's going to make her want to talk to me less if I do, I know I'd be downright pissed if someone woke me up in the morning by pounding on my door. Oh well.

I pound my knuckles against the door a couple more times and wait. After a couple minutes with no answer I decide to knock again feeling like I did all of this the day before. After standing on her front steps for over 10 minutes I figure she's not going to answer the door. And I can't say I blame her, even though it would make all of this a lot easier for me if she did.

After coming to the realization that she probably isn't going to answer her door anytime soon,

I walk back across the street and slip into my car. Instead of just driving off and calling it a day, I decide to wait for a while and see if either she or anyone else comes or goes from her trailer.

I know I'm being a major creep and would probably freak a bunch of people out if they saw me sitting here. But I figure, this is my best chance of seeing if she is home and is just refusing to answer the door or if she is actually gone. Thankfully the neighborhood is pretty much dead this morning so I don't have to deal with strange looks from people due to sitting in my car and staring at her house like a complete freak.

After a few hours of sitting in my car and playing on my phone, nothing has happened. And I mean nothing. No one has come or gone from her place and I've only seen one vehicle leave the neighborhood. I give myself another hour or two before I decide it's time to leave and face the facts that I am leaving with nothing more than I came here with.

Just as I'm about to start my car and pull away from the curb, I see the mail man opening people's boxes and delivering their mail. I watch as he gets to Sally's house and opens her mail box and leaves some envelopes in there, before turning around and walking back to his vehicle which is parked a couple homes down.

I slip down in my seat hoping he won't see me as he drives by on his way out of the neighborhood. I look in the rearview mirror and once he's gone I sit myself back up in my seat and look around. The neighborhood is still complete deserted and no one seems to be watching me from any of the parked cars or anything creepy like that. Not that I can talk at this point.

I feel like my only way to get answers at this point and to hopefully avoid going home empty handed is to break all of my moral laws and probably some real laws and look at her mail. I tell myself I won't actually open it so technically it's not a crime, at least that's what I tell myself in order to make myself open the door and get out of the car and make my feet move across the street towards her mail box. With a quick look over both my shoulders to make sure no one's watching I open her mail box and pull out the envelopes the mail man left.

I can't believe I'm doing this! I can't stop my mind from running a hundred miles a minute as I try to calm down enough to actually look at the envelopes in my hand. Quickly flipping through them shows me nothing, until I get to the last one in the pile and notice a different person's name on the address line.

After double checking that I'm not just seeing things I look at the name, Sally Yates, to see if I recognize it from anywhere. I can't seem to recall ever hearing or seeing that name anywhere before and the return address doesn't give me any information besides an address, with no company name listed anywhere that I can see. As quickly and calmly as I can, I put all the envelopes back in the mail box and turn around to make my way to my car.

Once I slump back in my seat, I try to catch my breath. Sometime between putting the envelopes back in the mail box and walking the 30 steps back to my car my breathing picked up and now I sound like I just ran a marathon instead of walked 200 feet. I mean I knew I was out of shape, but this is downright embarrassing.

After a couple minutes of heavy breathing I'm calmed down enough to pull out my phone and search the name "Sally Yates". Once it loads my screen is bombarded with results of a Sally Yates who was married to some wealthy lawyer who somehow ended up in prison.

Not really sure what I'm looking at or how any of this has to do with Brett, I keep scrolling until I come across an article with a name on it that I couldn't mistake. I drop my phone in my lap like it's on fire and will go up in smoke at any second and look away, like that will somehow make it un-true.

Nothing makes sense to me anymore, I don't understand what I'm looking at or what I found or how I've never heard of any of this before, but it clicks. Picking my phone back up I scroll and see that article after article tells me exactly what I need to know, followed up by pictures proving to my own eyes that it's true. My head doesn't want to believe it, but my heart knows what I'm reading is true and that Harmen has no idea what has been going on behind her back for years.

I put my car in drive and race out of the nasty neighborhood that holds the secrets that will tear my best friend apart. I am now more than ever dreading being the one that will have to tell her, but in the end this is why I came here. I wanted to find answers and I can definitely say I found exactly what I came here looking for. I just never thought it'd be this.

CHAPTER 16

Harmen

The last couple days I feel like I've been living on the edge, and not in a good way. I'm nervous all the time about doing or saying anything to set Brett off again. I still don't know exactly what I did or said that turned him into that man that left bruises on my arm. I woke up the morning after his freak out to find my upper arm covered in a bruise the shape and size of his hand. I tried to cover it up with makeup right away so no one would see it, but that just made it look worse.

So I've decided to where long sleeve shirts until it clears up, no one seems to have noticed which is all I really want. Thankfully it isn't too warm out because the last thing I want or need are people asking questions, especially Gray. It helps that I haven't seen him for a few days, so hopefully by the time I do it will be cleared up enough that I will be able to play it off or just keep wearing my long sleeve shirts.

Either way, I'll make sure no one sees it, not

because I'm ashamed, I just don't want people asking a bunch of questions and then deciding to dissect my relationship with Brett because I know that will just upset him more in the end. And that's exactly what I'm trying to stay away from, until I can decide what I want to do.

I keep telling myself I'm not scared of him and that I don't think he'll hurt me, that it was just a onetime thing. The problem with that though is I'm not sure who I'm trying to convince, especially since I haven't said any of it out loud.

I know Gray will be able to see past any lies I try to tell him, that's the only problem with having someone know you so well, I can't hide anything from him unfortunately. It's not that I want to lie to him or try hide it from him, I just know he will make it out to be something bigger than what it really is and right now I'm still waffling between what role I played and what part Brett played in this whole thing.

The last couple days he's thankfully been back to his normal self. He gives me hugs and kisses and tells me he loves me every day. Besides the first time he tried to touch me after the whole arm incident I haven't flinched at all, if that doesn't tell you I'm really not scared of him then I'm not sure what does.

He apologized the morning after too and we haven't brought it up since then. I see no point in reliving and rehashing the past if it's not going to happen again anyways. He promised over and over again that he didn't mean to hurt me, that he was just really upset and didn't know he was holding me that hard. When he apologized I've saw nothing but sincerity in his eyes, so I have no reason not to believe him at this point.

Most people would say I'm a very loyal person and some people probably see that as a flaw in times like this. I always say I will believe someone, especially those I care most about until they give me a reason not to. I know this may seem like a situation that should be enough for me to leave, but it hasn't happened before and he's told me it never will again. I guess you can say my loyalty has kicked in because I believe him and until I don't, I'm not going anywhere.

A big reason I'm trying to move past what happened is because he's been there for me since the day my parents died, so I can't let something this small pull us apart. I wasn't a good girlfriend following my parent's death, I know that. I was having a hard time coping with what happened and I ended up leaning on Gray for a lot of that, when I should have been leaning on Brett instead.

He's told me multiple times that it still hurts him that I didn't confide in him as much as I did Gray and I still find myself feeling guilty about that a little over a year later. So this time around, I'm going to go to him with my problems and he'll come to me with his, just like any couple in a healthy relationship would do.

After clearing my head, I get out of bed and

quickly get ready for the day. We only have two days left before we are supposed to be leaving for the trip that Brett has planned for us. I can't even explain how excited I am to get away from this place for a while.

I'll never admit it out loud, especially to Brett, but I do wish Gray was coming with. I know it'd be weird, but I've always wanted to go on a trip with my best friend, but I guess going with Brett will just be the next best thing. Like I said, I'll never admit that out loud, but that doesn't stop it from going through my mind.

Brett claims that he talked with all of my professors before booking the trip and notified them that I'd be gone for the rest of the week and the next so I don't have to do anything but pack. Since he still won't tell me where we are going it makes it kind of hard to decide what to bring, but I've decided since he won't tell me that I am just going to bring a little bit of everything and hope for the best. I mean at least this way, a couple of them should work.

A couple hours later once I'm almost done going through my clothes and deciding what I want to bring with, I hear the front door open and close. A couple seconds later I look up and see Brett standing in the doorway with an unreadable look on his face. He almost looks annoyed, but I'm not really sure. I try to remember if I did anything to cause that look on his face, but I can't think of anything off the top of my head.

Stepping into the bedroom he says, "Hey beautiful, so I have a question for you, but you have to keep an open mind okay?"

"Okay...," I answer hesitantly.

"What would you think about leaving a little early for our trip? I know it's short notice, but it'd give us a couple more days where we are going and since I already talked with your professors the only thing stopping us is you."

"Wait, you talked to my professors before you talked to me?"

"Yeah I just figured it'd make the decision easier for you if you already knew it was okay with them. Since they knew you weren't going to be in classes anyways it didn't seem like a big deal. I'm not trying to pressure you, but don't you want a little bit longer of a vacation? Come on, Harmen, live on the edge with me. Let's be spontaneous together," he says with a smile as he steps into the room and moves towards me.

There's something about his tone and this whole situation that has me on edge. Brett has never been spontaneous a day in his life, he and I both know it. So why now? I mean don't get me wrong I'd love to go on a longer vacation, but I can't help feeling like he's trying to push me into leaving early with him. I feel like lately I've been in a constant state of confusion, but there just really isn't another emotion to describe it.

Looking up I see his smile doesn't quite reach his eyes, it's almost like he's forcing himself to be happy about this. Why the hell would he want to leave early so bad if he's not even happy about it, doesn't make any sense to me.

Being honest with him I say, "Well I was hoping to see Gray quick before we left, just so I could say bye. I can see if he's around and maybe I could just stop and say goodbye to him before me left?" The moment I see his jaw tense up I know I said the wrong thing. Shit, he looks pissed.

Trying to pretend like I can't tell he's pissed off I continue to innocently say, "Or not? I don't have to if you don't think we will have time. I can just text him and tell him I'll see him when we get back."

Standing up as straight as he can he looks down at me and says with a snarl, "No. You don't need to see him or text him either. This is our damn trip and it has nothing to do with him. For once I thought you would be able to put our relationship first and be happy about what I'm doing for you, but instead you're more concerned with telling Grayson what's going on than just being happy with me. Un-fucking-believable."

Turning his back to me, he runs his hands through his hair and roughly pulls on the ends. I mean I'll be honest, if he pulls a much harder it looks like he could just rip it all out of his head and that just sounds downright painful and something I'd prefer not to witness.

I'm so used to reverting to sarcasm or jokes whenever I'm nervous or scared, but I don't think this is one of the best times for that. I've already seen when he can do and I'd hate to think it could be any worse, so I tell myself to rein in the sarcastic comments and hopefully I can come out of this unscathed.

When he turns back to me I can see a new sense of determination in his eyes and let me tell you it's freaking me out. Letting his hands fall back to his sides he looks me in the eyes and says, "Okay I think I've stayed silent long enough. This entire relationship has been about sidestepping yours and Grayson's friendship and I'm done doing it. You need to choose. It's either me or him, you can't have both the way you want to. You can have a boyfriend and a friend, but they are two very different things and you need to draw the lines."

Taking a deep breath, he continues, "You know I love you more than anything and that's why I'm doing this. For us. We need to be able to focus solely on us, no distractions. He needs to be able to find himself a relationship too and I think that's hard for him to do with how close you two are. This really is the best thing for everyone, Harmen. I haven't asked you to do it before because I know how much you need him, but I think it's time you start depending on me instead of him. I've been here since your parents' accident, I went through it all with you and I'm still here. I think that should tell you just how committed I am to you and this relationship, don't you think Harmen?"

I feel like my mind is racing a mile a minute.

Can I really separate myself from Gray? I tried it before and it nearly ripped my heart in half. It's been us against the world since we were little kids. Can I really change that now? I guess it hasn't really been us against the world since I started dating Brett though, has it.

I can't help, but still look at Gray as my other half even if he may not look at me that way. I think there's a part of me that's tried so hard to keep us close with the hopes that one day he will realize he loves me the same way I love him.

After high school and getting together with Brett I thought he may have realized he wanted me to be more than a friend, but over the last couple years I haven't seen or heard him say anything that would tell me he has. So I guess maybe it really is time to finally move on past that fantasy and focus on what's right in front of me.

I feel guilty hearing his words and knowing our whole relationship has been a way to pass time for me until Gray decides he wants to be with me. Maybe now really is the time to let go of that and move on with my life and the relationship I've been in for the last two years.

If my best friend doesn't look at me as anything other than a friend, then I think it's time that's how I start looking at him too. Am I really going to do this? Am I really going to separate myself from my best friend? Yes, yes I am. I'm going to do what I should have done a while ago, stop waiting around and finally take what I've had in front of me all along.

Looking at Brett I see a man who may never be the love of my life, but I've spent the last two years telling him I love him so now it's time I actually mean it, starting with this trip. I can do this, I can fall in love with the man whose been right I front of me for the last couple years, just like I should have done from the very beginning.

He may not be perfect, but let's be real, none of us are. I know now more than ever that the incident from a couple days ago was a onetime thing and something that I caused by not separating myself from Gray sooner. If it hadn't been for me focusing so much of my time on Gray, I never would have pushed him so far. In the end I know it's my fault, just like it's now my job to make it right.

Smiling up at Brett I say, "I'm so sorry. I never meant to hurt our relationship or chose my friendship with Gray over our relationship. If taking a step back from my friendship with him is what it would take to make you happy, then I'll do it. I'll focus on us, starting with this trip. I know I hadn't said it much, but thank you. Thank you for everything you've done for me since my parents' death and thank you for this trip and for putting us first, even when I haven't. But starting now, I will. Let's go on this trip and focus on nothing but us." I reach up on my toes and give him a kiss hoping it will reiterate everything I just said and the decision I made.

Settling back down on my heels I see all of the

tension and anger has left his face and is now replaced with a satisfied grin.

Smiling down at me he says, "That's all I've ever wanted. Thank you." He places a kiss on the tip of my nose and steps back.

"So now that we're on the same page, do you want to leave early? Say, half hour?" he asks with a mischievous smile.

"Half hour? Are you nuts? I just barely finished packing," I say while looking around trying to see if there's anything I missed and need to grab.

"No I'm not crazy, I'm being spontaneous, let's try it. And besides, you said you just finished packing so grab your stuff and let's go."

I can't believe I'm doing this, I'm a planner. I like plans. I'm not good with this whole spontaneous concept he's trying to preach. But what the hell, right?

"Ugh fine, you win. Let me just make sure there's nothing else to grab and then we can go," I say with a sigh and turn around to start collecting the last minute things I might need.

Before I can grab anything he lightly grabs my arm and turns me around. "What do you say we try something else too?" Oh good lord almighty, what else could he possibly want to do.

Crossing my arms, I ask, "What else do you want to try?"

"How about we both turn our cell phones off until we get there? I know it sounds crazy, but let's live in the moment. The only people we need are each other, so let's shut the world out for the day. What do you say?" he asks with a sly smile.

I know he can tell I'm hesitant because he continues, "Just for today, once we get there we can turn them back on. But just for today let's be together and focus on the trip ahead of us and on each other. Please?"

He's always the one who wants his phone on in case anyone from work calls him or even a client. But if he really is willing to do it, then I might as well too right? I guess this is the first step in the whole scheme of focusing on us.

"Okay fine, let's do it," I quickly answer.

He leans down and gives me a quick peck on the lips and turns away smiling, but stops a couple feet from me and to say, "Okay grab the last things you need, I'm going to grab a couple things then we'll get going." I give him a thumbs up and watch as he walks out of the room to grab his bags.

I quickly send off a text to Gray saying we are leaving a couple days early and that I'll let him know when we land. I can't cut him off cold turkey or who knows what he'll do. I'm still not too sure how he's going to handle my new found determination to put mine and Brett's relationship first and our friendship second, but I guess I'll figure it out once we get back home. Until then I'm not going to worry about it.

Seeing that the message sent I turn my phone off and stick it in the front pocket of my luggage and roll my bag to the door. It almost feels like a weight has been lifted off my shoulders by turning off my phone. I don't have to worry about anyone trying to get a hold of me or Gray sending me a bunch of messages. Instead, I get to focus on this fantastic trip, put together by the amazing guy walking towards me.

With a smile on his face he stops in front of me with his bags by his side. "You ready to go?"

I can't help the smile that comes on my face as I say, "Ready as I'll ever be." With one last look we are out the door and on our way to who the hell knows where.

CHAPTER 17

Grayson

After getting home from Los Angeles I wanted to give myself a day or so to find out anything else I could and then give myself the time to make sense of it all before I rushed off to tell Harmen. These aren't things I thought I would ever have to tell my best friend, but if I don't I know she will never know and I can't let that happen. She needs to know who she's pretty much sharing a home and a life with. She didn't go into their relationship hiding things that could ruin someone's entire life, but he did.

Brett went into their relationship knowing what he was doing and why he was doing it, unfortunately for my best friend she has no idea that she's been being used from the beginning. It makes me sick to my stomach every time I think about it and all of the signs I missed.

I call myself her best friend, but I couldn't stop this from happening or tell that something was off. I let this go on for over two years and that's on me. I've always told myself that I will protect her and look out for her no matter the cost.

Since her parents' death I knew it was just me, I

was all that was left to take care and look after her and I feel like I've let them down by not stopping that monster sooner.

My phone dings on the coffee table next to me pulling me out of my internal rant, I grab it and I see it's a text from Harmen. Just seeing her name hurts from everything I have to tell her, but not knowing how to do it just makes it that much harder.

Opening the message, I read it unsure of how to respond. "Hey Gray! Change of plans we are leaving tonight for our trip instead of this weekend. Sorry I couldn't see you before we left, it was a last minute thing! I'll let you know when we land. Bye!"

Dropping my phone onto the table like it's on fire I stand up and start pacing in front of the couch, not knowing what to do.

I never should have waited this long to tell her, I should have told her as soon as I got back. But then I know she would have started asking questions that I didn't know the answers to and I would have felt even worse about the entire thing. At least now I have answers that may help put her mind at ease, or at least as much as possible given the situation. I just have to find a way to tell her before they leave.

Grabbing me phone off the coffee table I rush out the door towards my car and call Harmen's cell phone. No answer, not even a ring. What the hell! Did she turn it off? Why would she do that though, she never turns her phone off in case I need to get a hold of her, which is very much what I need to do right now.

I call again and again like a crazy person thinking that by some miracle it will turn back on one time. No luck. I send her a quick text telling her not to leave until I talk to her and step on the gas.

Flying through town and swerving around various vehicles to try get me to her place faster probably makes me look like a lunatic to anyone who doesn't know the gravity of the situation. I keep one hand on the wheel at all times and the other on my phone calling her over and over again just waiting for that one call to go through.

Frantically I pull up outside her building and dash out of my car as soon as I put it in park. I take the stairs two at a time up to the second floor where her apartment is and pound on the door.

"Harmen, open up I need to talk to you," I yell as I continue to bang my fist against the door.

"Harmen, come on please it's really important," I yell trying to get across my need to speak to her.

After what feels like a couple minutes of frantically pounding and yelling at the door, the neighbor from across the hall taps me on the shoulder. I instantly stop my fist from hitting the door again and turn around to face the old man who looks royally pissed off.

"Would you shut the hell up already! She's not home for Christ's sake can't you tell. So take your loud noises away from my apartment or I'll call the cops," he says.

"What do you mean she's not home? Where'd she go?"

"I mean what I said boy, she's not home. It's not that hard to understand."

"Do you know where she went? Did she say where she was going?" I ask frantically.

"Slow down boy, I don't know where she went or any of the other questions running through that head of yours. The man just said they had to hurry or they'd miss their flight. That's it, that's all I know. Now leave me alone," he says with a huff.

Before I could ask him anything else he was already closing his door in my face.

Brett was already here with her? Did he try pressure her into leaving early cause he found out I went to see Sally? Oh Lord please tell me that's not the case or I have a feeling this is going to get a lot worse before I get a chance to talk to her.

Raking my hands through my hair I roughly pull on the ends so hard I'll probably have a bald spot, but I'll put some miracle grow on it later and it'll be fine. Flight.

He said something about catching a flight. Before I can think of anything else I take off towards my car and make my way back to Los Angeles, knowing that it's the closest airport. Guess I'm going back to where this whole thing started and hopefully this time I'll be able to put an end to this charade once and for all, but only if I catch them before they leave.

CHAPTER 18

Harmen

I have to say, the couple hours it takes to get to L.A.X from Mitchell definitely feels like it is taking forever without a phone. Usually I would be looking at all the different apps I have, playing games or even listening to music. Instead we have been talking about anything and everything the entire time so far and I have to say I absolutely love it. I can't help but feel like I'm missing something or like someone needs me for something, but I'm on vacation now and that means I don't have to worry about it.

Brett seems to become more and more relaxed the closer we get to Los Angeles, which is probably just because he's feeling the same way I am. But I can say that nothing is better than that feeling you get right before you leave for a vacation. No worries or responsibilities in the world, nothing but sunshine and water to look forward to. Well hopefully that's what I get to look forward to, I guess it could be the tundra or even the jungle since he still hasn't told me where we're going.

I'm usually not a very spontaneous person, but so far I'm loving it. I may not know where we are going or how long it'll take to get there, but I do know wherever it is it'll be amazing because Brett wouldn't book us anything less.

Looking over at him I try to grill him one more time since I have nothing else to do. "Will you tell me where we are going now? Jungle? Hawaii? Antarctica? Come on, just give me one hint. That's all I want."

"Fine, I'll give you one hint. But that's it."

Bouncing up and down in my seat and clapping my hands together like I'm a little kid I turn towards him with a big smile on my face and wait for my hint.

"We're going somewhere you've never been before. That's all I'm telling you," he says with a smile while still keeping his eyes on the road.

Throwing my hands up in the air I turn back and face the road with a huff, "I've never been anywhere besides home and Los Angeles. You know that. So that's a bull shit hint."

"Hey you never said it had to be a good one. A hint's a hint," he says with a chuckle. I just glare at him as if that'll get him to tell me, yeah right.

After a couple minutes Brett breaks the silence by asking, "Do you want to stop? The rest area is a couple miles up and we can get out, stretch our legs and use the bathroom. Is that alright?"

"Yeah that's fine, I could use the bathroom

anyways."

Brett pulls his sports car into the parking spot closest to the doors and puts it in park a couple minutes later. We both get out and stretch our legs and make our way to the separate bathrooms in the building a head of us. Obviously as a girl I take a little longer than he does, by the time I finish drying my hands I walk out of the building and see a couple people gathered around Brett's car.

I start walking towards the group of people and as I get closer I hear shouting. Instinctively I know this is something bad so I run up to the group of people and push a couple of them aside until I can get to the front of the group and see what's going on.

You know how some people say the universe works in mysterious ways? Yeah I totally believe that. Why else would I be looking at Gray pushing Brett up against the side of his car with a look of pure murder on his face? How did he find us and what the hell is he doing here? Those are the first things that pop into my mind.

Instead of running to try pull him off of Brett and demand some answers I can't seem to move my feet. It's like my feet and my brain just decided they no longer wanted to communicate with each other at this point and have decided they didn't want to give me a heads up. I can't do anything but stand and watch this unfold until they start communicating again.

All I can see are the two of them deep in conversation and a sly smile spread across Brett's face. Looking at Gray, I see a completely different expression written on his face, anger. So much anger. I've never seen him look so angry before in my life. Yes, of course I've seen him mad but this is to a whole other level.

His face has a tint of read to it that just keeps getting darker and darker and I'm guessing it has to do with whatever Brett is saying. I'm pretty sure smoke would be coming out of his ears right now if it were possible.

His arms look like they're shaking, either from anger or from trying to hold down Brett I can't quite tell. The biggest thing that catches my eye is a pieces of paper that he seems to have clenched in his hand. He lifts them up to show Brett and I watch in slow motion as whatever is on those papers transforms him right before my eyes.

All the color drains from Brett's face and he looks at the papers like he's seen a ghost. What the hell is on those papers that would make him react that way.

After what feels like an eternity of watching this unfold from the sidelines my feet finally decide it's time to move. I let my legs carry me across the remainder of the parking lot and up to the two men in my life to figure out what the hell is going on.

Running up to them I try to pull Gray off of Brett and separate them, which is definitely easier said than done. Once Gray sees it's me trying to pull him off he steps away right away looking completely defeated. "Does someone what to tell me what the hell is going on," I yell at them.

I watch as Gray turns and looks towards Brett who is pale and his face is currently blank of any expression. He stands up taller as he looks over at him and asks, "Do you want to tell her or should I?" I turn to look at Brett who won't meet my eyes and wait for his answer.

Running my hands through my hair I ask myself what the hell is going on? Those seem to be the only words my brain can form right now. With a big sigh I realize there are only two people who can answer that question for me and it turns out they're both right in front of me.

I let my arms fall to my side and turn towards Brett looking for answers. "Well are you going to tell me what's going on or is he going to have to?" I ask him while pointing over my shoulder at Gray.

After a couple seconds of him still not meeting my eyes, I know whatever it is that Gray confronted him about is not something I will enjoy hearing. When he still wasn't talking I decided to give up hope of hearing it from the source and turn towards the man who seemed to hold all the answers.

"Fine, if he's not going to tell me, then you do it. Just tell me what's going on," I plead with him. "Please Gray," I whisper.

CHAPTER 19

Grayson

This is not how I was hoping to do this, not if front of people and not in front of him. I wanted to tell her these things in private where she could ask any questions she wanted to and I could try help her figure out the answers. But now as luck would have it. we have the source of all of our problems right here and I know he's not going to be too forthcoming with her.

It's taking everything in me not to kill him right now for all of the things he just confessed to me. Now all I can hope for is that he at least has the decency to admit them to her as well.

Closing my eyes and taking I deep breath I turn towards Harmen and try to work up the courage to open my mouth and deliver the news that's going to break her. Opening my eyes, I find her watching me with conviction, like she hopes I hold all the answers for her, and thankfully I think I do. I can do this.

With one last deep breath I start to tear her

world apart. "I'll start from the beginning. Do you remember when I told you I went to see Brett at his office a couple weeks ago? And do you remember the flowers he gave you right before that? Well I left some parts out."

With a sigh I continue, "I was the one who gave you the flowers, I was trying to get back on your good side after the fights we'd had, but when I never heard from you I started to get confused. Then when we met up a couple days later and you gushed about the flowers Brett had given you I knew something was up. What I told you about going to his office to clear the air was true, but what I didn't say was that he admitted to taking the flowers and giving them to you from him. I also didn't tell you that he threatened to ruin our friendship, and I didn't tell you because I knew I'd never let that happen."

With a short pause I watch her look at Brett for confirmation, she must get what she was looking for when he still won't meet her eye because when she looks back at me I see nothing but anger on her face.

I figure since I started this I better finish it so I continue, "You know I've never liked the guy and after that I took it upon myself to find out everything I could about him."

Before I continue I need her to understand that I never wanted to keep any of this from her, I can't lose her once she hears it all. "Before I say anything else, I need you to know I never wanted to keep any of this for you and I only put it all together yesterday, but I was too scared to go to you and tell you right away. I know it was a cowardly thing to do, but I need you to know I just want you to be happy and safe. That's all I've ever wanted," I plead with her to believe me.

"That's fine Gray I get it, but I need you to tell me what else you're talking about right now. No more waiting," she scolds me.

With a deep breath I continue, "Like I said after that I wanted to find out everything I could about him, so I looked at his file in the college system. I noticed there was a different birthday then what you've told me his was and there was a completed transcript from a law school in Los Angeles along with a completed transcript for an undergraduate degree from a different school. On top of that it looks like he was never taking classes at Peskin to begin with. His transcript shows he enrolled for classes but dropped them all at the last minute."

This is a lot harder than I thought it would be, but I need her to know everything so I continue. "I kept looking and came across a woman he had listed as his emergency contact. From what you've told me about him before I knew he didn't have any family left, or at least that's what he told you."

I shoot Brett a look and notice he's staring at the ground acting like he's ashamed and he knows I haven't even gotten to the worst part.

Tearing my eyes away from him I look back at Harmen and continue on to some of the worst parts. "I tried to call the number he had listed for her and she answered. I talked with her for a couple minutes, but as soon as I mentioned Brett's name she froze and hung up. I couldn't help but feel like I was missing something and I couldn't figure out what had spooked her so bad. So, I drove to L.A. the next day to try speak with her in person. When I got to her place, which by the way was probably in the most run down and unkempt part of the city, she didn't seem to be home. I knocked again and again hoping she would come to the door, she never did. When I was going to leave I saw an old man watching me and decided to ask him if he knew her. He got upset with me and accused me of being there to take her way. I didn't understand what he was talking about, but he kept going on and on about some younger man in a suit coming and yelling at her and threatening to take her away if she didn't listen to him."

I sigh running my hands through my hair, letting out a big breath and dropping my arms to my sides as I continue the story. "I left feeling confused and came back the next day to find out she still wasn't home. Or if she was, she'd been too scared to talk with me. I sat outside her home for a while hoping to catch her coming or leaving, but that never happened. But, after a while the mail was delivered to her house, I know I shouldn't have but I wanted to make sure she was okay since most people stop their mail if they're out of town for a few days. I checked her mail box to see how much mail had piled up and notice there were only a couple things, on the top was an envelope with the name, Sally Yates, on it."

As I continue I watch Brett become more and more agitated out of the corner of my eye. "On the paper I found at the college he had written down the name, Sally Long, so I wasn't sure who Sally Yates was. I went back to my car and decided to search the name hoping something would come up, and it did." After taken a couple deep breathes I look at Harmen and hope that she can see in my eyes that I'm not lying about this.

"According to multiple sources and all the articles I read, Sally Yates was the wife of business-man, Jeff Yates, and they had a son named Brett Yates. It still didn't make much sense to me. All of the articles talked about how Jeff's longtime business partner turned him in for stealing from their company. He is now apparently in federal prison spending time behind bars because of it. This happened over 15 years ago and his wife ended up divorcing him and taking back her maiden name, Long."

Before I can continue Harmen cuts me off frantically waving her arms in the arm like she doesn't know what to do with them.

"What does that have to do with me? And what does that have to do with Brett?" she asks and I can tell the minute she understands where

I'm going with this story.

She looks at Brett with a confused expression on her face, when he won't meet her eye she turns back to me.

"Please tell me his last name isn't Yates," she pleads with me.

Looking at the ground, unable to meet her eyes I shake my head and say, "I can't do that. I'm sorry Harmen."

I look up at her and see tears rolling down her face, I want nothing more than to wipe them away, but I know they will just continue to fall as I finish what I have to say.

Clearing my throat and showing her one of the pictures in my hand, I continue, "I found this picture of their family from before Jeff was sentenced to prison." While she's looking at the picture of what looks like a perfect family, I can tell she recognizes the younger boy in the picture as Brett. She lets the picture fall to her side and starts walking closer to Brett.

Before I can stop her she's in his face pleading with him to tell her why. I pull her against my chest before she can do anything to him and tell her there's more to the story, which causes a sob to escape her mouth.

Holding her to my chest I force myself to tell her the rest before I can stop myself. "I found out he changed his last name after his father went to prison and his mother took back her maiden name. But I still didn't understand why he wouldn't just tell you any of this until I found a picture of Jeff Yates with his old business partner, the man who turned him in. I'm sorry Harmen, it was your dad."

I pull out the other picture I have from my back pocket, one of Harmen's father and Jeff Yates posing together in front of their business.

With shaky hands she grabs it and looks at it, while choking on a sob. She turns and looks at me in confusion. "Why would my dad not tell me he had a business partner? I never heard him or mom talk about him having one. Ever since I can remember they always talked about it as dad's business and never mentioned anyone else, especially a Jeff Yates. I don't understand."

"I didn't either right away that's why I dug a little more. It looks like your and Brett's fathers started the business together a long time ago. When your dad found out Jeff was stealing from the company he turned him in and took his name off of everything associated with the company. After that it was like Jeff was never a part of the business to begin with. That's why you never heard about it, it seems like he tried to forget it happened and just wanted to move on."

Before I can say anything else, Brett is pushing me away from Harmen.

He forcefully grabs her by the arm and yells in her face, "Your fucking father took everything from us, from me. He stole my dad, my mom, our money. Everything. Your father was a fucking liar who decided he didn't care about any of us enough to do anything besides throw us away. He never would have been able to start that business without my dad's help, yet in the end he took my father's name off of everything which left my mother and I with nothing. Do you know what it was like growing up having everything to only have it taken away from you? No of course you don't because you grew up living the life I should have had. The life my mother and I deserved."

In slow motion I watch as he throws her to the ground and delivered a swift kick to her stomach and bends over her to deliver his last blow. "And you know what I did to make it right? I killed them. That's right, I killed your parents to make them pay for everything they ever took from my family. And I did it to take it all away from you so you could see what it felt like to lose everything you ever had. Hiring someone to mess with their vehicle was the easy part, having to listen to you bitch and whine for months on end was the hard part. I knew the only way to get back everything my mother and I deserved was to get it through you, so I did what I had to and would have kept doing it until the day you had access to the trust your parent's left you. Then I was finally going to get rid of you once and for all."

Turning towards me he continues, "but you had to go and fucking ruin it! All of it down the drain because you couldn't keep to yourself. This was supposed to me my week to get everything I ever lost back. I was going to get rid of her sooner because you couldn't keep to yourself and decided to go sniffing around in our business. You left me no choice but to move everything up and take care of it quicker It's your fault all of this happened!"

"You killed her parents! You took them away and that wasn't good enough? You needed more?" I yell at him.

In slow motion I watch as he puts a hand around his back and brings it back around with a gun in tow and points it directly at me with a satisfied glint in his eyes.

Feeling the air rush out of my lungs I throw my hands in the air to try show him I'm not a threat. "Come on Brett, put the gun down. Don't do anything you're going to regret," I try to plead with him.

With a completely humorless laugh and menacing smile he says, "You don't get it, I don't regret anything besides not getting my money sooner. Fucking Nick was supposed to have papers to me before we left that would give me the rights to the money in the case of her death. But since he's even more of an idiot than you, I don't think that will be happening. So the next best thing will be taking away the last thing she cares about. You. I promise it'll be over soon, don't worry."

Before he does anything I look down and Harmen and give her a soft smile and say to her with everything in me, "I'm so sorry, I didn't mean for it to turn out like this. Just know I love you and I promise I always will. You've always been it for me, never forget that."

Closing my eyes, I turn my head to look back at Brett and hope when I open them he won't go through with it. When I open my eyes I see what my ears apparently couldn't hear, flashing lights. Looking around I see that a number of police cars have pulled into the rest area and are parked with their guns drawn on Brett. One of the people watching this whole thing unfold must have called them.

"Drop the gun," one of them yell at him and I see the moment he realizes he has nowhere to go, with one last smile he points the gun back at me and pulls the trigger.

As I fall to the ground all I can think about is how much I love the woman who is laying on the ground a couple feet away and that I can't reach her one last time, before everything goes black.

CHAPTER 20

Harmen

I hear a loud bang followed by watching Gray's body fall lifelessly to the ground. "No!" I yell through sobs as I try to move towards him.

This can't be the end. It can't be. He just told me what I've spent almost my entire life wanting to hear, he can't be gone. Before I can move more than an inch I hear another shot ring out causing me to drop my head to the cold concrete and try to protect myself from any more bullets that might come.

After a couple seconds of silence, I hear officers shouting orders and people running to the now two lifeless bodies on the ground. Brett. They shot him, and all I care about is getting to my best friend before they can take him away from me.

As I'm trying to move I'm stopped before I can get anywhere by medics trying to look me over, but I can't tear my eyes away from the ghostly white frame of my best friend as he's surrounded by officers and medics trying to save him.

Save him. I always thought I would be the one to save him if the time ever came, now look at me. When he needs me most I can't even get to him.

"Please be okay. Please be okay," I whisper to myself and I watch the medics load him into the back of a nearby ambulance.

Once he's out of sight I feel my body go lax and let everyone around me do their jobs. I feel them put a collar around my neck and gently lift me onto a flat board. It's hard to feel anything but numbness as they lift me off the ground and into an awaiting ambulance. Once the doors are shut, we take off and all I can do is close my eyes and pray that when I open them this was all have just been a bad dream.

Waking up cold and alone is the first thing I notice. I open my eyes slowly and take in my small hospital room, there's nothing but my bed, a chair and all the equipment in here. Completed with beige walls and all, I lay back in my bed realizing it wasn't just a bad dream like I hoped it was.

It all comes back, slowly flooding my mind in a whirlwind that makes me feel like I'm either going to be blown away or drown in all the events that took place. I don't know how long I've been in here or how long I was asleep, but it doesn't feel long enough. I try placing everything I remember in order of how it happened to make sure I'm not missing anything. The thing that keeps playing on a loop in my mind is Brett's confession to me.

He killed my parents. The man I had spent the last two years with killed them. How could I not know? I guess the answer to that is simple, I didn't know just like I didn't know he was lying about who he was. I used to think of myself as a smart girl, one with a lot of common sense, but now I question that and everything else about myself.

I get that my dad wanted to hide what happened between him and his old partner, but I just wish he would have thought to tell me about it. At least just mention it, I never would have judged him or looked at him any differently. He was still the father I loved with my whole heart, he just had a secret he decided to keep that unfortunately came back to affect me.

As mad as I want to be at him for never telling me, I can't because he's not here anymore. He's not here anymore because Brett decided to take matters into his own hands and punish me for something I knew nothing about. I just can't believe I didn't notice anything sooner. I can't help but feel like my parents would be disappointed in me if they were still here. Just thinking about him and what he has done brings bile to my throat.

I finally remember everything that happened causing me to frantically search for a call button to get a nurse in here. Gray. What happened to Gray? Is he okay? Did he die? A million questions are running through my head as an older nurse walks through the door.

"Oh good looks like you're awake, how are you

feeling?" she asks sweetly.

"I'm fine. Can you tell me what's going on with my friend Grayson Beck? Is he here? Is he okay?" I find myself wincing at the pain in my side.

"Breathe honey, you have some bruised ribs that are going to cause some pain if you get yourself all worked up, your friend is okay. I just came from checking on him and he made it through surgery but he's still asleep, that's all they really know. And his family is on their way," she smiles at me sadly and pats my hand as she checks all the machines around me.

I wait till she's done checking me over before I ask if I can go see him. She finally relents after my 100th time of asking. I tell her once I see him for myself I'll come back to bed and rest.

Finally, she relents and loads me into a wheel chair and steers me down the hall to his room. She reminds me over and over again that he still isn't awake and that he's going to look kind of ruff from where he hit is head when he fell to the ground. She also told me that he was shot in the chest and will be in quite a bit of pain when he does decide to wake up.

I keep repeating to myself that he's okay. I'm nervous to see him and see how he looks, but my heart is more concerned with making sure he's okay with my own eyes. It's like my heart knows it won't fully recover from everything I've learned if I'm not able to see him.

Thankfully this batty old nurse was willing to bring me down to see him or I'm afraid they would have found me dragging my machines behind me while walking down the hallway just so I could check on him. I know I'm desperate, but I don't care.

With one last warning she pushes me through his door. My breath catches in my throat as I look at my best friend lying limp in the bed. He looks so helpless and broken, I did that to him. It hits me like a ton of bricks when I realize he's here because of me. He could have died because of me. I know he always thought it was his job to protect me, but I never thought he would have to go this far to do so.

The nurse rolls me up to his bedside and tells me I can hold his hand if I want. Knowing it's okay to do so, I hesitantly reach out and grab a hold of his hand laying closest to me, making sure I'm careful not to mess with any of the wires attached to him.

"I'll give you guys a few minutes," the nurse says as she pats my shoulder and walks out the room.

Softly holding his hand in mine I move my thumb over the top of his in a soothing motion. I'm not sure if he can feel it or if he knows I'm here, but I hope he does. I've never talked to someone while they lay in front of me unconscious, even when I came to the hospital to see my parents after the accident I didn't talk to them, I just couldn't do it.

It killed me inside to see my lively and loving parents lay lifeless on a bed and there was nothing I could do to help them. But with Gray, I feel like I need to talk to him and let him know I'm here for him, even if he can't hear me.

While rubbing his hand I find myself quietly confess what I've always been too scared to say out loud. "Hi Gray. I'm so sorry I did this to you. I should have seen the signs that something wasn't right a long time ago. It shouldn't have taken you being in danger for me to realize it and I can't apologize enough for that. I can't forget what you said to me before it all happened, you said you love me. I don't know if you meant it as a friend or if you see me as something more, but it doesn't matter to me because I'll always love you no matter what, even if it's only ever as a friend. But I want you to know that I do love you as more than my best friend, I'm in love with you and I always have been. I can't let anything happen to you without telling you. You're it for me and you always have been. I convinced myself for so long that I could be with Brett and be happy even if he was never the one I wanted. As long as you were in my life in some capacity that's all that mattered. But now after everything that happened, I can't help but tell you that you are everything to me, you're my best friend, my partner in crime, and I know you're the love of my life. I promise I will finally force myself to tell you all of this if you wake up, but if you can hear me now just know that I do love you and I always will."

I lean down and press a kiss to the back of his hand and lay my head on his arm, while his bed soaks up all the tears I can't seem to stop. I keep my head down and resting on his to bring myself the only comfort I can of being by his side, until I feel his hand tighten around mine.

You'd think I heard another gun shot or something by how fast my head snaps up.

I look him over from head to toe to see if he really moved or if I just imagined it. Ever so slowly I see his lips pull up into a small smile before I hear him softly say the words I've only dreamed of hearing.

"I'm in love with you too."

EPILOGUE

Grayson

Three Years Later

Ten years ago I never would have pictured my life where it is today. I knew from the very first day I met Harmen that I would always have her in my life. I just never knew for sure in what capacity that's be. As I grew up, so did she and I started to want more from her. I missed my chance once and I told myself after that, if I ever got the opportunity again, I would grab her and never let go.

So here I am three years later watching my wife and one-year-old son play on the floor of our home. I always knew she was an amazing woman and I had no doubts she would make an incredible wife and mother, but I was not prepared for just how great she would be. It makes me love her more if that's even possible.

I truly don't think anyone come be prepared or comprehend what becoming a mother does to a woman, especially one as incredible as her. She has devoted the last year of her life to our son and making sure he is happy and cherished at all times, no questions asked. She always says she wants our son to look at us the way she always looked at her parents. She strives every day to make them proud while they watch down on us and I don't think they could be anything but.

Above and beyond that, she treats our marriage the same way. First and foremost, we are still best friends and partners in crime, obviously not real crime or anything, we aren't that crazy. But we promised each other on our wedding day that we would always look out for and protect each other no matter what, no questions asked. And that's exactly what we've been doing every day since then.

After the incident with Brett three years ago, everything changed for us. We no longer played around the bush or sidestepped what was right in front of us. We committed to each other and haven't looked back since.

One-year after Brett was shot and killed by officers in the rest area parking lot, I got down on one knee and asked her to marry me. I wanted to change the way she looked at that day going forward, I wanted her to have something good to remember instead of all the terrible memories that day brought her.

We didn't want to wait to get married, call us impatient. So with the help of my family we put together a small intimate ceremony and got married only a couple months after my proposal. A little over a year after that we welcomed our son, Hudson Brian Beck, into the world.

She often says she's able to look at him and remember her father. She has long forgiven her father for the secrets he kept from her and now only looks back with fondness. We remember her parents as the kind and loving people they were and how they protected Harmen the way they thought was best for all those years.

Even though what he hid might have ended up causing her pain, in the end she knows why he did it and understands why as a parent he would want to keep such negative things out of the house and away from her. We both know he never would have kept it from her if he thought for a second or would have known the damage it could cause, but that's the price you pay for trying to protect those you love. Sometimes it works out how you hope and other times it doesn't.

You live and you learn, that's what my parents always taught me and that's what we will always teach our children. Protect those who are closest to you no matter the cost. You win some, you lose some. Not everything you do it going to be right or perfect, but if you truly believe in why you are doing something then at least you won't regret it in the end.

Looking at my family now, I don't regret anything that happened. I just wish I could have saved her the pain she suffered at the hands of

Brett, but you can't change the past, only the future.

Harmen and I may have taken a long time to come together how we always should have been, but I wouldn't change it for the world. I never dreamed of my wife being my best friend and I can honestly say it's that greatest thing that's ever happened to me.

As if she knows what I'm thinking, like always, she looks up at me with a loving smile and I know no matter where life takes us we can handle it, together.

The End